HUBRIS

A lost boat, a stray girl, and a gutted salt faze Scottish police

PETE BRASSETT

Paperback published by The Book Folks

London, 2020

ISBN 978-1-913516-16-1

www.thebookfolks.com

HUBRIS is the eleventh novel by Pete Brassett to feature detectives Munro and West. Details about the other books can be found at the end of this one. All of these books can be enjoyed on their own, or as a series.

Prologue

Unlike the residents of nearby Girvan and Stranraer whose urban existence was sullied by the constant distraction of noisy bars, clubs, and restaurants, neds on joyrides, and the piercing wail of police sirens, the denizens of Lendalfoot – an all but isolated coastal farming community with barely enough houses to qualify as a village – lived with their senses attuned to the rustle of the leaves on the trees, the bleat of a stray lamb, or the tell-tale signs of an impending storm.

Mindful of waking his wife, Willy Baxter, a wiry, sixty-two-year-old with hair as rusty as his favourite sweater, slipped from the comfort of their bed, made his way downstairs, and zipped his coat to the collar, safe in the knowledge that by the time he returned there'd be a roaring fire in the hearth and the house would be filled with the welcoming aroma of a full, fried breakfast and burned toast.

Relying on instinct rather than the beam of a flashlight, he made his way across the sodden field towards an abandoned stone bothy where the youngest of his flock, a mix of blackface and Cheviots, would be waiting for their feed, the half-mile trudge made all the more arduous by the driving drizzle and the biting south-westerly battering his back.

Distracted by the familiar sight of a ship's beacon, he cupped his hands around his eyes in an effort to focus on the pulsating light, perturbed not because it appeared larger than usual, nor because, against the sinister silhouette of Ailsa Craig rising from the waves, it seemed brighter than usual, but because, unlike the other trawlers, container ships, or cruise liners that crossed the firth, it was completely stationary.

Forsaking the lambs to satisfy his curiosity, he made for the shore where, with the sound of the diesel engine rumbling beneath the roar of the wind, he stood, hands in pockets with his hood billowing about his head, mesmerised by the stricken wreck.

With its blue, timber hull, white wheelhouse, and worn rubber tyres lashed to the prow, the boat – a twenty-eight footer, listing on the rocks – was what many a landlubber would describe as 'charming' or 'traditional', but for a bemused Baxter, the fact that a fishing vessel could stray off-course and run aground with the nearest harbour just four and a half miles to the north was utterly inconceivable unless, of course, a soul had perished on board.

With scant regard for his own safety, or the rheumatism in his shoulders, he yanked his phone from his pocket, called the coastguard, and waded waist-deep into the icy water, cursing as he struggled to drag himself onto what appeared to be the Celtic equivalent of the Mary Celeste.

Half-expecting to find the skipper slumped at the helm with an empty bottle of rum by his side, Baxter, whose experience of boats was largely limited to availing himself of the bar facilities aboard the Arran ferry, was astute enough to realise that the glowing computer screens and the incessant beep echoing around the cramped confines of the bridge, was evidence enough that the navigation system was functioning as normal.

Returning to the open deck, he made his way aft and, shuddering at the swell of the sea, concluded that the crew, short of abandoning ship for no apparent reason, must have been swept overboard unless, by some bizarre twist of fate, they'd become trapped in the hold.

Dropping to his knees, he slipped a finger beneath a round, brass catch, raised the hatch to the cold store beneath and, by the light of his phone, peered inside where, had the excursion been a fruitful one, he'd have been greeted by the sight of threshing mackerel or a haul of pollock. However, despite being as hard as a slab of Galloway granite, what lay before him was enough to make him scramble for the stern and heave the remnants of last night's supper over the side.

Chapter 1

No longer reeling from the emotional turmoil of a broken engagement to a gamophobic toff whose serial philandering had not only driven her to contemplate opening a vein but also, as a direct consequence, transformed her once burgeoning career into a car crash waiting to happen, Charlotte West, following a serendipitous encounter with DI James Munro whilst on secondment to the East End of London, was acutely aware that were it not for her senior's size twelve constantly pounding her backside, she would now be in rehab or, worse still, six feet under.

On his return to Caledonia, Munro, recognising that she'd yet to fulfil her potential and would doubtless, without the necessary guidance and support, spiral into oblivion, had cajoled her into transferring north of the border where, under his watchful eye and burdened with a sense of responsibility, she finally repressed the urge to spend her evenings downing copious amounts of cheap vodka and falling face first into a half-eaten kebab and had, instead, risen through the ranks to become a confident, if not impetuous, Detective Inspector.

With Munro convalescing from heart by-pass surgery and enjoying his retirement in the company of Murdo, a rescue dog with whom he shared a passion for beef and a dislike of vegetables, she was able to divert her attention away from 'Jimbo', her mentor and father figure, to concentrate on the job in hand.

* * *

Unlike her former self, who would have needed nothing less than a 7.2 on the Richter scale to rouse her from her slumber, West, now armed with more *carpe diem* than an ornamental fish pond, was ready to go when, at precisely 5.35am, she received a call from DS Duncan Reid informing her that he was on his way over.

Clad in her favourite black jeans, white tee shirt, and waxed biker jacket, West, who chose to spend her disposable income on essentials like steak, wine, and chocolate, rather than fritter it away on needless frivolities like cosmetics, finished her make-up routine, which comprised smearing a dab of cherry-flavoured balm across her lips, tucked her hair beneath her cap, and dashed across the rain-soaked courtyard to the waiting Audi.

'This is a first,' she said as she slipped into the passenger seat, 'blokes are normally dragging me into bed at half-five in the morning, not out of it.'

'Oh, the joys of a misspent youth,' said Duncan with a grin, 'we've all been there.'

'Who said anything about youth? I'm talking last Tuesday. So, what have we got?'

'Bacon,' said Duncan, handing her a roll, 'brown sauce, and a body in a boat.'

'Must be the catch of the day. Where is it?'

'A few miles south of Girvan.'

'So, how do we get there?' said West as she demolished her breakfast. 'Have they got a chopper for us, or do we have to row out?'

'No, no,' said Duncan, 'if we did, I'd not be here. You forget. Me and boats, separated at birth.'

'Oh yeah, I forgot, you're no Captain Pugwash, are you?'

'Well, can you blame me? If you remember, the last time I was on a boat, it was with yourself, and it nearly turned into a submarine.'

'Don't exaggerate,' said West, 'it was only a force nine, no big deal.'

'Well, this one's on the rocks, so it's going nowhere. Oh, and your pal McLeod's already there.'

'Pathologists, eh? Where would we be without them?'

'Aye, right enough, every home should have one. Have you heard from the chief?'

'Jimbo? Yup, we had a chat last night,' said West. 'He's doing fine and if you asked me, I'd say it was all down to that dog.'

'How so?'

'It gives him a sense of purpose. You know what he's like, he can't sit still for a minute. At least now he's got the dog to look after, he won't be interested in what we're up to.'

Duncan turned to West, scratched the stubble on his chin, and smiled.

'I'd not count on that,' he said as he fired up the engine. 'Mark my words, once he gets a sniff of this, he'll be back, just you see.'

* * *

With the biting south-westerly gaining strength and a raft of thunderous, black clouds threatening to unleash a deluge of biblical proportions, the atmosphere on the beach, bar the eerie glow of flashing blue lights, was as dark as the sky above.

Duncan, whose image was contrived to help him blend effortlessly amongst life's more unsavoury characters, buttoned his beaten leather car coat, pulled his woollen watch cap low over his brow and, in his tatty jeans and scuffed boots, approached the constable with his arm outstretched like a jakey on the beg.

'Alright, pal?' he said, waving his warrant card. 'What's the story?'

'Don't ask me,' said the dour-looking officer, nodding towards the boat. 'I'm just directing traffic, if any shows up.'

'Well, who's in charge?'

The constable shrugged his shoulders as a tall, hooded figure wearing a white Tyvek suit appeared like a spectre on deck.

'Duncan!' said McLeod, hollering above the roar of the wind. 'Where's Charlie?'

'Right here,' said West. 'You alright?'

'A wetsuit wouldn't go amiss but apart from that, aye, not bad. And yourself?'

'Couldn't be better. Permission to come aboard, captain?'

'Granted. But you'll be needing a suit first.'

'What? In this weather?'

'Suit. The pair of you.'

* * *

Looking not unlike the mascot of a well-known tyre company, Duncan, stressing the seams of his coveralls, wedged himself in the doorway of the wheelhouse while West, swivelling on the pilot's chair, regarded McLeod with a mild look of amusement as his head skimmed the ceiling.

'Well, this is fun,' she said, wincing at the audible beep in the background. 'I've never played sardines on a boat before.'

'Dear, dear. You're not claustrophobic are you, Charlie?'

'Only in certain company. Can we turn that blooming thing off?'

'I'd not do that,' said Duncan, 'not yet anyway. It's probably the GPS or something. Best leave it for someone who knows what they're doing.'

'Why?'

'I don't know. Maybe it's got some sensitive information on it?'

'Alright,' said West, 'good point, I suppose. So, do we know any boffins with a nautical bent?'

'Oh, wake up, miss, you've been working with Dougal long enough. He's fishing daft, you know that.'

'Of course he is. Sorry, it's just that every time you mention his name, I keep thinking of Brains from *Thunderbirds*, that's all.'

'Well, he's on his way over,' said Duncan, 'but he'll not be here in a hurry, not on that wee scooter of his.'

'In that case,' said West, 'we may as well press on. Andy, any idea who's in charge here?'

'Aye, it's a Sergeant Miller,' said McLeod. 'He's in the squad car.'

'Really? What's he doing there? Afraid of getting his uniform wet?'

'Actually, he's having a wee chat with the fella who called this in, a chap by the name of Baxter. He spotted the boat from over the way, there.'

'That's a bit suspicious, isn't it? I mean, what the hell was he doing out here at this time of the morning? In this weather?'

'He's a farmer.'

'Oh. Fair enough. Okay, we'll have a word with him later. Can you fill us in on anything, now?'

'All I know,' said McLeod, 'is that this fella, Baxter, saw the boat, called the coastguard, then hopped on board.'

'Why?' said West. 'Surely any sane person would've stayed on dry land?'

'He's a local, Charlie. He knows what can happen out here. From his point of view, the only reason this boat could've ended up here, is if there'd been an accident. If somebody was injured.'

'And were they?'

'All in good time.'

'So, what happened next?'

'The coastguard secured the vessel and killed the engine.'

'Hold up,' said West, 'you mean the motor was still running?'

'Apparently. It's not a bad thing as it happens, that's basically what's kept it on the rocks.'

'All a bit odd, isn't it?'

'Which is precisely what Baxter thought. He assumed the crew had toppled overboard. In fact, the chopper's somewhere out there now looking for anyone bobbing about in a life jacket.'

'Then what?'

'Then he took a wee peek in the cold store.'

'And what did he find?'

'Have you had your breakfast?'

'Only a bacon roll.'

'Then you should be fine.'

McLeod led them to the stern of the boat, lifted the hatch to the cold store, and directed the beam of his hand-held searchlight into the hold.

'Down there,' he said. 'I'm warning you now, Charlie, it's not a pleasant sight. It's not pleasant at all.'

Chapter 2

West, having discovered a freezer full of body parts on her very first assignment with Munro, was unperturbed by anything McLeod had to offer and cast him a sideways glance before peering into the hold.

Overwhelmed by a morbid curiosity and fascinated by what was undoubtedly one of the most bizarre spectacles she'd ever witnessed in her entire career, she took the torch from his hand, dropped to the deck and, lying flat on her stomach, lowered her head beyond the hatch for a closer look.

Male. Roughly five feet, seven inches tall. Dark brown hair. Bushy beard. Stocky but not muscular. Naked from the waist up. Wounds: two. The first, a deep, clean incision running from the neck to the groin. The second, approximately ten inches long, running across the torso at right angles to the first.

Lowering her right arm, she gently pulled the puffy, milky-white flesh to one side and was surprised to see, through a shallow pool of blood and body fluid, what appeared to be the vertebrae of the spine glinting in the torch light.

'Bloody nora!' she said. 'It's like he's been… what's the word?'

'Gutted?' said McLeod.

'Well, it is a fishing boat,' said Duncan, 'par for the course, if you asked me. Jump up, miss, give us a wee look. What's he missing?'

'Most of the lower bits and bobs,' said McLeod. 'I can't say exactly from up here but it looks like the stomach, pancreas, liver, kidneys, intestine, that sort of thing.'

'Oh, that's a beauty!' said Duncan. 'No prizes for guessing where that lot ended up.'

'Right enough. It must have been a fair old feeding frenzy for the fishies, that's for sure.'

'Best keep Dougal away from this. He'll pass out on the spot.'

'The question is,' said West, 'why? I mean, killing someone is easy enough, but why unzip them like a sleeping bag?'

'I deal with the *hows*, Charlie,' said McLeod, with a smile. 'The *whys* are your department.'

'Well, give us a *how* then. For example, how did another bloke manage to fit down there and slice him open?'

'He didn't,' said McLeod. 'That fella sustained his injuries up here, then he was tossed below deck.'

'Gives a whole new meaning to the phrase "down the hatch". Got a weapon?'

'Aye, it's a fisherman's knife. It's down there, next to the body.'

'I saw it,' said Duncan, getting to his feet. 'It's double-edged, about four or five inches long.'

'Correct,' said McLeod. 'One side of the blade is smooth, that's used for making an incision in the flesh; the other side is serrated with a wee hook at the end, that's used for ripping out the guts.'

'Eloquently put,' said West. 'I don't suppose there's much else you can tell us just yet, is there?'

'Not until I've done a post-mortem, but that won't take long. Whoever did this has saved me a couple of hours' work.'

'And do you think whoever it was, has experience of gutting fish?'

'I'd not take that as a given, Charlie. A knife's a knife. No experience necessary.'

'So, the only question left for now,' said West, 'is where's the perp?'

'He could be anywhere,' said Duncan. 'Assuming he's the one who scuppered the boat, he could have made off on foot, maybe even had a car waiting.'

* * *

West perched on the side of the boat and, scratching her head through the hood of her suit, stared pensively into the void below as Dougal, wearing an open-face helmet, a nylon windcheater, and waterproof leggings, called from the shoreline.

'Are you wanting me up there?' he said, wiping the rain from his goggles. 'Only, it looks a wee bit slippery.'

'Aye, get yourself suited and booted,' said Duncan, 'and hop aboard. This is right up your street.'

Unlike Duncan, whose sartorial style had all the elegance of a penniless hobo, DS Dougal McCrae – who preferred to conduct his investigations from the comfort of a warm office rather than the great outdoors – took great pride in his Italian-inspired appearance.

Tutting despondently at the state of his sodden, suede desert boots, he swapped his designer anorak for a set of coveralls, made a note of the boat's registration emblazoned on the bow, and clambered aboard.

'No, no!' said Duncan, raising his arms. 'That's far enough!'

'How so?'

'Because if you see what's down here, you're liable to have yourself a cardiac, and I've not got the defibs with me! What you're after is in the wheelhouse.'

Excited by the sight of three small computer screens, the largest no bigger than an average iPad, Dougal immediately pulled his phone from his pocket and snapped the displays to capture their final settings as Duncan and West squeezed into the cabin behind him.

'Jeez-oh!' he said without turning. 'Have you seen this lot?'

'Seen one, you've seen them all,' said West. 'What's the big deal?'

'That,' said Dougal, pointing to the monitor farthest away, 'is a dedicated fish finder – sonar, if you will. It'll pick up large shoals of fish so you know exactly where to drop your line.'

'Line?'

'Aye, this is a fishing boat, miss. It's not a trawler. And this one here, is what we call a chartplotter. It's GPS, no different really to the sat nav in your motor but it also connects with the NMEA to monitor wind speed, direction, that kind of thing.'

'Riveting.'

'But this,' said Dougal, beaming like a kid in a sweetshop, 'this is the jewel in the crown. It's a standalone AIS unit.'

'Which is?'

'AIS. Automatic Identification System. It's how ships track and identify each other.'

'So why is that so special?' said West. 'I mean, couldn't they just use a pair of binoculars?'

'It's special, miss, not because of the price, and they cost a wee fortune, but because I'd never expect to see a model like this on a boat this size.'

'How not?' said Duncan. 'Is that not just a normal bit of kit for these sailing fellas?'

'It is, aye. Even the chartplotter has a basic version installed as standard, but this is much more sophisticated. This is top-end, best of gear. It's for larger vessels on the open sea.'

'Well, what's that out there,' said West, pointing towards the window, 'if it's not the open sea?'

'No offence,' said Dougal, 'but there's a world of difference between the Clyde and the middle of the Atlantic, miss. And there are regulations too, and that's what makes this all the more unusual.'

'What regulations?'

'Like the one that says a boat this size should never be more than twenty miles from a safe haven.'

'That's all very well, pal,' said Duncan, 'but you know what folk are like, they get a bit carried away, sail a bit farther than they should.'

'Aye, maybe so, but to have this on board means they didn't do it on a whim. Wherever they went, they went there intentionally, and what I don't get is why they'd leg it and leave an expensive piece of kit like this behind.'

Beginning to wish she'd joined a sailing club as a wean rather than spending her weekends grooming ponies at the local stables, West, frustrated by her ignorance in matters of a maritime nature, groaned as her patience wore uncomfortably thin.

'The fact that they've left it behind is neither here nor there,' she said brusquely, 'what matters is whether it's any good to us!'

'Aye, it is!' said Dougal. 'More than you know! It has data back-up, which means we'll be able to find out exactly where she's been and what course they took.'

'Never mind where it's been!' said West. 'I want to know where it came from!'

'Calm your jets, miss! That's easy. It's local. Dumfries.'

'How do you know?'

'The registration on the prow: DS155. The "DS" means Dumfries is the official port of registration.'

'That's the chief's territory,' said Duncan. 'I told you he'd get involved.'

'We're keeping him out of it,' said West. 'I've told you already, no excitement for him, not so soon after his by-pass.'

'I'll ring around and see where it's berthed,' said Dougal, 'it'll not be far, Garlieston or Stranraer, maybe. So, what's going on out there? I'm guessing you've not found a great white in the hold?'

'No, no,' said Duncan, 'just a body. Mind you, he looks as if he's gone ten rounds with one.'

'I'm not with you.'

'Let's just say, he's like a taco with no filling.'

'That's plenty,' said Dougal. 'Miss, are you okay?'

Annoyed by the lack of pockets in her Tyvek suit, West leaned against the door, folded her arms, and scowled at Dougal.

'Not really,' she said. 'This is doing my nut in and we've not even started. I mean, an RTC is one thing, I can handle that, but what the bleeding hell do we do with a boat?'

Dougal helped himself to the swivel chair and flashed her a reassuring smile.

'It's easy, miss,' he said, 'just a slightly different procedure, that's all. The first thing we have to do is inform the MAIB, that's the Marine Accident Investigation Branch. It's not a big deal, their job is limited to establishing the cause of the accident. Once they've done that, then that's them away.'

'Cheers, Dougal. At least someone knows what we're doing. And after that?'

'The same as usual. Obviously we need SOCOs, but it's not possible here. I mean, they'll not even get a tarpaulin up, not in this weather. We need a crane, a low-loader, and an escort. The nearest harbour is Girvan, they've a couple of covered slipways and a dry dock. I'll call the harbourmaster now and sort something out.'

'You,' said West, 'are a diamond! Right, you deal with that while we have a word with this Baxter geezer.'

* * *

Sergeant Miller, with his greying hair and a complexion which suggested he'd spent most of his life pounding the beat with nothing for company but a packet of cigarettes and a whisky-filled hip flask, barely flinched as West and Duncan flung open the doors and leapt into the front seats.

'Alright?' said West, smiling as she flashed her warrant card. 'DI West, and this is DS Reid. Sergeant Miller, I presume?'

'Aye, that's me.'

'And you're Mr Baxter?'

'The one and only.'

'Have you a first name, Mr Baxter?' said Duncan. 'Titles seem a wee bit formal in situations like this.'

Baxter, swathed in a silver space blanket, smiled and nodded gently.

'Willy.'

'Smashing. So, Willy, how are you bearing up?'

'Aye, not bad. In fact, I'm getting quite toasty, now. I've not worn one of these before.'

'The miracles of modern science. You should get yourself a couple, they're not dear.'

'Is that so?'

'Aye, might be useful if you're out in all weathers.'

'Quick question, Sergeant,' said West. 'Have you informed the marine investigation people, yet? About the boat?'

'Not yet,' said Miller, 'I've been sitting with Mr Baxter here, he's had quite the shock.'

'He's not the only one by the looks of it. I take it you've seen the body, too?'

'I have indeed. It's a rare sight, I'll give you that.'

'And are you okay?'

'Nothing a wee brandy couldn't fix.'

'Good,' said West, 'well, we won't keep you long. Willy, I'm sure your missus must be wondering where you've got to.'

'No, you're alright. I telephoned her earlier, she knows what's happened. Truth be known, I'm more concerned about the sheep. They'll be wanting their feed.'

'Then we'll be as quick as we can. Why don't you just talk us through what happened this morning.'

Baxter pulled the blanket tight around his shoulders and settled back in his seat.

'It's really quite simple,' he said. 'I was on my way over to feed the sheep when I saw the beacon on the boat, so I came down for a look.'

'Why was that?' said Duncan. 'I mean, you must see boats out here all the time, what made this one so different?'

'It wasn't moving. And the beacon was bright – too bright to be out in the firth.'

'Okay, go on.'

'Well, it was juddering about on the rocks. I figured for it to end up there, there must have been an accident, so I jumped on board. Got myself a right soaking into the bargain, too.'

'And there was no-one there?'

'Not a soul. Which was odd. That's when I thought maybe they'd tumbled overboard.'

'Why's that?' said Duncan. 'I mean, I know it's blowing a hoolie out there, but it's not that bad, not for folk who sail these things.'

'Right enough, Sergeant, but who knows what it's like beyond the firth. That thing could've bobbed for miles on the tide, I don't know.'

'Fair enough. So, with no-one on board you had yourself a wee look in the hold.'

'I did. I had a wee look in the hold, and then I lost my supper.'

'Can't blame you for that,' said West. 'Is there anything else you can tell us? For example, did you see anyone wandering about? Anyone walking down the road? Any cars? Another boat, perhaps?'

'No, that's it,' said Baxter. 'No folk, no cars, no boats. Just the poor fella down below.'

* * *

Dougal, sitting astride his scooter with the engine running while McLeod struggled to keep his umbrella from taking him on a parascending adventure along the beach, sounded the horn as Duncan and West stepped from the patrol car.

'I'm away up to Girvan, miss,' he said. 'Dr McLeod's going to wait for the MAIB then follow the low-loader up to the harbour.'

'Aye,' said McLeod, 'I've arranged for an ambulance to meet me there. If you need to get a hold of me after that, I'll be at Crosshouse.'

'Blinding,' said West. 'All we have to do now is find out who actually owns this tub.'

'You need to take yourselves off to Kirkcudbright,' said Dougal. 'That's where it has a berth. The fella you need to speak to is Sandy McCain, he's the harbourmaster.'

'Nice one, Dougal, cheers. Duncan, do you know where this Kirkwotsit is?'

'Aye, miss, it's a way down the coast. It'll take at least an hour for us to get there.'

'Good, then we'd better get a wiggle on. That way we can have lunch when we arrive.'

Chapter 3

With long, unsociable hours, low profit margins, and the ever-present risk of disease amongst the livestock, a farmer's lot is seldom rewarding. But for Willy Baxter, who shunned intensive factory farming methods in favour of allowing his animals to lead as normal a life as possible, the added anxiety of being married to a woman whose temperament wavered between the docility of a dormouse and the unbridled rage of a deranged Doberman, was enough to drive him to distraction.

As a smitten twenty-two-year-old, the newly-wed Maureen Baxter had spent her days tending to the neeps and tatties, carrots and cabbages, and beans and broccoli she'd lovingly planted in the sprawling vegetable patch to the rear of the house whilst her evenings, despite her husband extolling the virtues of the local supermarket and the Indian restaurant, comprised a never ending cycle of cooking, cleaning, and baking.

However, with the passage of time, what was once an enjoyable daily routine in a rural idyll had fast become a perpetual round of tedious chores made bearable only by the occasional tipple and an unhealthy intake of Tunnock's teacakes.

Keen to rinse the taste of bile from his mouth and wipe the image of a disembowelled carcass from his mind, Baxter dropped his coat to the quarry-tiled floor, kicked off his wellies, and hung his head in despair as her voice began grating on his ears before he could make it up the stairs to the sanctuary of the bathroom.

'At last!' she said as she scurried towards him. 'Just where the hell have you been? Ten minutes, you said! Ten minutes! And that was nearly two hours ago!'

'Aye, well, it took longer than I thought.'

'Eleven times I called! Why could you not answer? Could you not have picked up even just the once?'

'I was busy.'

'So, who was the fella in the boat? What was all the fuss about?'

'For Christ's sake, Maureen! Give me peace!'

'Did you see the police? Were they asking questions?'

'Aye,' said Baxter, pulling off his sweater. 'They were asking questions, but not as many as you.'

'And Rhona? Did you tell them about Rhona?'

'Would it have been so bad if I had?'

'You didn't?'

'I did not. I said we lived alone, just the two of us, shackled together in wedded bliss.'

'Good,' said Maureen, lowering her voice. 'We don't want folk snooping around when what she needs is some peace and quiet.'

'What she needs,' said Baxter, gritting his teeth, 'is to tell us just what the hell is going on instead of hiding away like some kind of a recluse! She's thirty-one years old! She's a grown woman!'

'And she's your daughter! The least you can do is show some compassion!'

Baxter placed one foot on the stairs, grabbed the handrail, and cocked his head at his wife.

'And why's that?' he said. 'Why should I show her compassion?'

‘Because she’s lost her job, and she’s lost her flat, and she needs our help.’

‘Give me strength! You’re in denial, Maureen! Wake up and face the facts!’

‘I don’t know what you mean.’

‘Rhona’s lost her job, has she? She’s been told to leave the flat, has she? Then tell me this, why did she pitch up here in the dead of night with just a handbag and the clothes she’s standing in? Where’s her belongings? She’s not even brought a suitcase with her!’

‘She… she had to leave them behind.’

‘Why? That’s right, Maureen, you’ve all the questions but none of the answers. Three weeks she’s been here. Three weeks and she’s not even left the house. She doesn’t watch the television, or listen to the radio, or even read the newspaper! She doesn’t even have her computer with her! The only time she comes up for air is when there’s food to be had!’

‘It’s not her fault,’ said Maureen, ‘she has stuff on her mind.’

‘There’s something not right here and she’s not saying. Well, I’m telling you this, I’ll not put up with it much longer.’

‘You listen to me, Willy Baxter, you leave her be, do you hear? She’s… she’s depressed.’

‘Is she, by Christ? And why’s that? Because she’s not yet a captain of industry with a six-figure salary?’

‘Aye! And because she shouldn’t have to sleep in the cellar!’

‘It’s not a cellar, it’s my den!’

‘It’s underground!’

‘Aye, it’s underground,’ said Baxter. ‘And it has a carpet, and heat and electricity, and a TV and my books, and it’s where I go to escape!’

‘Escape from what?’

'From yourself, Maureen! Yourself! I'm away to freshen up. If you see that daughter of yours, tell her to get off her backside and start looking for a job.'

'Tell her yourself,' said Maureen, 'you've probably woken her with all your shouting!'

'See here, Maureen. I'm trying my best not to lose my patience with you, so I suggest you take yourself off and have some of your medicine before I lose it altogether.'

'What medicine?'

'The one with "Glenfiddich" on the label!'

* * *

Baxter cleaned his teeth and eased himself into a steaming hot bath where he lay with his eyes closed, knowing full well that by the time he reached the kitchen there'd be a breakfast on the table and his wife, having indulged in a snifter, would be full of the joys of spring.

Troubled by his daughter's irrational behaviour, particularly as, with a raft of qualifications, a decent job, and a doting partner, she appeared to have the world at her feet, he dismissed a tiff with her boyfriend as insufficient grounds for her unexpected arrival and concluded that she was probably going the way of her mother.

Angered by the lack of privacy and with it, the opportunity to gather his thoughts, he cursed as Maureen interrupted his musings with a ferocious knock on the door.

'Willy!' she said as she knocked again. 'Willy! Are you listening?'

Baxter took a deep breath, opened his mouth, and considered slipping beneath the surface.

'Aye, go on,' he said. 'What is it, now?'

'It's Rhona! She's not in her room! She's gone!'

Clad in just a towelling robe with bath water running down his legs, Baxter, tempted to follow the aroma of bacon sizzling in the pan, stopped by the door to his den and turned to face his wife.

'What did you say to her?' he said, trying to remain calm.

'I've not said anything!'

'Well, you must have said something to make her leave.'

'I did no such thing! I was making yourself some breakfast and I came to see if she wanted some too, but she wasn't here.'

Baxter, assuming his wife to be making a whisky-inspired mountain out of a molehill, padded down the stairs and glanced around the room where, aside from the light still burning, and the duvet neatly folded on the sofa, everything appeared as normal.

'What will we do?' said Maureen. 'Willy, what on earth will we do?'

'Did she not leave a note? Upstairs, maybe?'

'No. I've not seen one.'

'Well, perhaps she's taken herself off on a walk. God knows, she could do with the exercise. And the fresh air. Does she have her phone with her?'

'I don't know.'

'For heaven's sake, woman! Did it not cross your mind to call her before flying into a panic?'

'No!'

'Well, call her now!'

Maureen dialled the number and held the phone aloft, her face blanching at the sound of her daughter's voice requesting she leave a message.

'Perhaps she called a taxi,' said Baxter.

'No, no,' said Maureen, shaking her head. 'I'd have seen it leave.'

'Not if it picked her up at the bottom of the lane, you wouldn't. What about her boyfriend, this Callum fella?'

'She said we're not to call him.'

'I don't care what she said, try him now! Perhaps she's gone home. At last.'

'And what will you do?'

'I'll take a wee drive,' said Baxter, heading for the kitchen. 'If she's only just left, then she'll not be far, unless she's away up the woods. Then again…'

'Then again, what?'

'If she left at two in the morning, she could be anywhere by now.'

'And if you don't find her?' said Maureen. 'What happens then?'

'Well, if she's not with Callum,' said Baxter, 'we'll call the police. There's nothing they like more than a missing person, especially a depressive with delusions of grandeur and an alcoholic mother.'

Chapter 4

Blessed with a metabolism which enabled her to burn more calories than a thoroughbred on Derby Day, West, sporting an enviably slender figure, scoured the harbour in search of a café as the sound of rigging clattering against the masts filled the air.

'I fancy a burger,' she said. 'A big, bloody burger with tons of ketchup.'

'I wonder why,' said Duncan. 'Will you be wanting some raw liver to go with that?'

'Right now, I could chew the hind legs off a donkey.'

'Not that I'm wanting to put you on a diet or anything, miss, but do you not think we should take care of business first?'

West considered her options and nodded.

'Yeah, I suppose so,' she said. 'But let's make it snappy, I'm wasting away here.'

* * *

Expecting the harbourmaster to be a wily old seadog in a white, knitted sweater and black fisherman's cap, West was disappointed to find Sandy McCain, a clean-cut forty-something, seated behind a tidy desk, looking as average as a bank teller.

'Are you Mr McCain?' she said, proffering her warrant card. 'The harbourmaster?'

'I am, indeed. And yourself?'

'DI West, and this is DS Reid. I wonder if you can help.'

'I'll do my best, Inspector. What is it you're after?'

'A boat.'

'Well, you've come to the right place,' said McCain, grinning sarcastically. 'Kirkcudbright's the busiest harbour in the whole of Dumfries, and we've a marina, too. So, is it any boat you're after, or have you a particular one in mind?'

'Fair play,' said Duncan, smiling back. 'You'll be needing some detail, then. It's the *Thistledonia.* Registration DS155.'

'I know it well,' said McCain. 'That's Tam McClusky's boat.'

'Can you tell us anything about it?'

'There's not much to tell. It's a boat. A thirty-two footer. Good condition. He runs it as a charter vessel.'

'Sorry,' said West. 'I'm more of a land girl myself. What exactly do you mean by charter?'

'He hires it out, with or without a skipper. Tourists mainly, on fishing trips, although a fair few locals use it, too. Those deluded enough to think they'll land a tiger shark or some such beast.'

'And these charters, are they… what then? Day trips?'

'No, no,' said McCain, 'longer than that. Most folk will take the boat for a week or so. Ten days, maybe.'

'And do they go far?'

'Far enough. The most common trips are across to Ireland, or up the way towards Mull or Skye. You should speak with Tam, he'll know more than me, that's for sure.'

'No danger of a number, is there?' said Duncan. 'Only, we're in a bit of a hurry.'

'No need,' said McCain, 'you'll find him across the street, he's in the café.'

'Now that,' said West, 'is what I call perfect timing. What's he look like?'

'Oh, you'll not miss him,' said McCain. 'He's a big fella. I mean, big.'

* * *

With the tourist season well and truly over, and the locals thin on the ground, the café, save for an elderly gent reading a newspaper and someone resembling a silverback in an ill-fitting sports jacket, was empty.

'Tam McClusky?' said Duncan. 'DS Reid, and this is DI West. Have you got a minute?'

'Take as long as you like,' said McClusky. 'I'm in no hurry.'

'It's about your boat, the *Thistledonia*.'

'Oh, aye?'

'I understand it's a charter.'

'It is, but if you're after renting it, then you're out of luck. She's not back yet.'

'We know,' said West. 'That's why we're here.'

McClusky leaned back, narrowed his eyes, and glared at West with a look of curiosity.

'London?' he said. 'What's a London lass doing up here?'

'Actually,' said West, 'it's Berkshire.'

'Berkshire? Is that not what they call "the stockbroker belt"? All silver spoons, pin-striped suits, and privileged educations?'

Having spent her teenage years carousing with the ne'er-do-wells in the less salubrious parts of the county where alcoholism, homelessness, and drug abuse was as rife as the capital, West was often willing to forgive most people their naïve if not misguided perception of her birthplace, but in McClusky's case, she made an exception.

Armed with a tactic she'd mastered for disabling opponents twice her size – a technique which, contrary to popular belief, did not involve a swift kick to the nether regions but relied instead on the bending back of the fingers until a loud crack was heard – she deemed McClusky an ignoramus who posed no threat at all.

'You need to get out more,' she said. 'There's only one thing worse than an old fool, and that's an ignorant one.'

McClusky locked eyes with West, held her gaze, and smiled.

'I think we'll get along, you and me,' he said. 'We're cut from the same cloth.'

'Good. Just as long as we understand each other. Now, do you fancy a brew?'

'You're alright,' said McClusky. 'I'm just about done.'

'Suit yourself. Just give me a minute.'

West turned to the counter, collared the waitress, and ordered two mugs of tea, two burgers, and a plate-load of French fries before taking a seat.

'Sorry about that,' she said. 'Right, about your boat.'

'What about it?'

'We've found it. In fact, we're hanging on to it.'

'Finders keepers?'

'Something like that.'

'Are you not telling me why?'

'See here, Mr McClusky,' said Duncan, 'before we go into any detail, there's a few things we need to know first, so you'll just have to bear with us, okay?'

'Go on.'

'We need to know who you rented it to, how long they took it for, and where they were headed.'

'No bother,' said McClusky. 'They're regulars. They take her out every six weeks or so.'

'They?'

'Aye, there's two of them.'

'I don't suppose one's a short-arse, by any chance?' said West. 'About five-six, slightly podgy, brown hair, beard?'

'No. They're two of a kind. Lanky fellas. Skinny. Red hair. Why?'

'No reason. So, have you any idea where they went?'

'That's not my business,' said McClusky, 'but they usually head west, south-west.'

'Ireland?'

'Maybe.'

'Is that not a bit far?' said Duncan. 'I mean, is there not some sort of regulation that says your boat can't be more than twenty miles from dry land?'

'Right enough, Sergeant. You're well-informed, I'll give you that, but here's your wake-up call. It's only twelve miles or so to the Antrim coast from Southend, and from here, the trip across to Bangor's not much more.'

'That's me told. Every six weeks, you say? That's a lot of holidays. How do they pay?'

'Cash.'

'And do they work?'

'I've no idea,' said McClusky, 'but they enjoy their fishing. You should try it some time, it's very relaxing.'

'So is a pint of lager in front of the football,' said Duncan. 'Can we have their names, please?'

'Jack and Henry Boyd.'

'Brothers?'

'Aye.'

'Where from?'

'Moffat.'

'We need an address,' said West, 'and a telephone number, if it's not too much trouble.'

McClusky glanced sheepishly at West, pulled his phone from his pocket, and scribbled a number on a paper napkin.

'No bother,' he said, as he slid it across the table. 'That's Jack, he's the fella I deal with.'

'Nice one,' said West. 'So, tell me, when exactly are you expecting them back?'

'Yesterday,' said McClusky, sniffing as he ran a finger over his pock-marked nose. 'That's why I'm sat here instead of putting a line on at the bookies.'

'So, they're bit late, then?'

'It happens. Especially if the weather turns, but right now I'm thinking maybe they've been delayed because somebody's commandeered my boat.'

'Maybe,' said Duncan, 'but unlikely. It was beached a few miles south of Girvan. I'm afraid you'll not be seeing it for the foreseeable.'

'How so?' said McClusky. 'I've got bookings.'

'All I can say,' said West, 'is that there's been an incident. Until we make some headway in the investigation, we can't tell you any more than that.'

'What you mean is, there's been an accident.'

'An incident.'

'Has the boat been damaged?'

'Like I said. Sorry to be the bearer of bad news, but if I were you I'd get on the blower and cancel those bookings.'

'I'd best call the insurance people, too.'

'The Marine Accident Investigation Branch will let you know what happened.'

'Well,' said McClusky as he hauled himself to his feet. 'There's no point in me hanging around here, then. I'd best see what's running in the three-thirty, then give the boy the bad news.'

'Sorry?'

'My son. He's not been well. We'd planned a wee trip across to Port William but no boat, no trip.'

'Too bad,' said West. 'Before you go, I need your phone number and an address, just in case we need to get in touch.'

McClusky opened his wallet and tossed a business card onto the table.

'Call me anytime,' he said. 'Enjoy your lunch.'

* * *

Deeming a burger unfit for human consumption if accompanied by anything green, West, gagging at the sight of a limp lettuce leaf lurking beneath the bun, tossed it to one side and replaced it with a generous dollop of red sauce and a spoonful of mustard.

'So,' she said as she took a bite, 'what do you think?'

'I'm not with you.'

'McClusky. Animal, mineral, or vegetable?'

'Vegetable,' said Duncan. 'Did you not clock his ears? He's half man, half cauliflower.'

'Hardly surprising. A bloke his size with that attitude, I bet he's had a few punch-ups in his time.'

'Aye, right enough,' said Duncan. 'I wonder what he did for a living.'

'Professional meathead by the looks of it.'

'Well, he's past it now. He must be sixty-odd at least. Still, at least he was pleasant enough.'

'It's a front,' said West.

'How so?'

'I can tell. He's got a thing about the police.'

'Everyone in Scotland has a thing about the police. No, no, I shall have to disagree with you there, miss. If anything, he's got a thing about women.'

'How d'you mean?'

'Old school,' said Duncan. 'He feels threatened if they're not in the kitchen obeying orders.'

'Yeah, maybe.'

'So, what now?'

'Fudge brownie,' said West. 'Then we'll give this Boyd geezer a bell, and if he doesn't answer, we'll shoot up to Moffat.'

'Did you not want to check on the chief while we're here?'

West pondered for a moment and shook her head.

'Nah, I've had second thoughts,' she said. 'Best leave Jimbo in peace for now, at least until we've got this sorted.'

Chapter 5

As a typical Taurean who approached her investigations with all the finesse of a bull in a china shop, West, being as stubborn as a mule, did not hold with the belief that there was a right way and a wrong way of tackling any particular task. It was just her way, or none at all.

Seething at still having to occupy the passenger seat when she knew in her heart of hearts that she could handle any vehicle better than a tactical pursuit driver, she finally succumbed to the pleasure of having a chauffeur and began to enjoy the opportunity it afforded her to absorb the sights and sounds of a part of the country she'd not seen before.

As a year-round destination for hardened hill walkers eager to explore the Sir Walter Scott Way, ogle at the Grey Mare's Tail, scale Gallow Hill, or scoot down the Devil's Beef Tub – a hollow in the landscape once used as a hiding place for cattle pillaged from English farms by the lowland reivers – the old spa town of Moffat, formerly a thriving centre for the woollen industry, boasted several hotels, numerous cafés, and a plethora of quaint shops which served as the perfect backdrop for the hordes of camera-wielding visitors to the area.

Duncan, eyes peeled for a parking space, crawled along the high street, stopped opposite the Annandale Arms, and watched as West, rather than follow his lead, headed towards the tearoom, the toffee shop, and the ice cream parlour.

'Wrong way, miss!' he said, as he chased after her. 'Star Street! It's just there!'

'Hold your horses,' said West. 'Do you fancy a raspberry ripple?'

'In this weather?'

'I'll take that as a no, then.'

'We'll get one on the way back, let's go before it starts pelting down.'

* * *

The house, located in the upper reaches of a narrow, winding lane, was a converted stable block with living accommodation on the upper level whilst the lower, with a timber barn door opening directly onto the street, served as a garage and a workshop where the Boyds were busy hosing the dirt from a mud-encrusted 4x4.

Tickled by the sight of the flame-haired siblings wearing matching anoraks and thick-framed spectacles, West slackened her pace, smiled at Duncan, and elbowed him in the ribs.

'Bloody hell!' she said, grinning. 'It's the bleeding Proclaimers! *And I would walk five hundred miles, and I would walk–*'

'That's plenty!' said Duncan. 'No offence, miss, but you've not got the accent. Or the voice. Alright lads? Which one's Jack, and which one's Henry?'

'Who's asking?'

'DS Reid. And this is DI West.'

The elder of the two turned off the hose and glanced furtively at his brother.

'I'm Jack,' he said. 'Is there something you're wanting?'

'Just a wee word, if it's not too much trouble. It's about your fishing trip.'

'Oh, aye? What about it?'

'Tam McClusky. He says you're quite the regular with him.'

'Maybe.'

'How often do you charter his boat?'

'Now and then.'

'You need to be more precise than that,' said West. 'How often?'

'Once a month,' said Jack. 'Five or six weeks, maybe.'

'That's a lot of time off. Doesn't your boss mind?'

'We've not got a boss, we work for ourselves.'

'Budding entrepreneurs, eh? So, what do you do, exactly?'

'This and that.'

'I said exactly.'

'Labouring,' said Jack. 'Building work, repairs, fixing stuff.'

'I assume you keep your books in order, then?'

'Aye. I do it myself. We've no need for an accountant.'

'Good for you. Let's hope for your sake you won't be needing a lawyer either.'

'This trip of yours,' said Duncan, 'when did you leave?'

'The fourteenth.'

'So, ten days ago. And what time did you set off?'

'Around three.'

'That's a bit late, isn't it?' said West. 'Not much daylight left.'

'Three *am*,' said Jack. 'We went with the tide.'

Duncan, head bowed, walked slowly to the front of the 4x4, sucked his teeth at the sight of the dented bumper, and wandered back again.

'You're not saying much, Henry. What is it? Laryngitis?'

'I know my rights,' said Henry. 'I'm not obliged to say anything, not unless you arrest me, and even then, only if I want to. And only in the presence of a solicitor.'

'You know your stuff,' said Duncan, 'I'll give you that. So, you've got a choice, pal. You could try being a bit more co-operative, or if you prefer, we can do it your way and arrest you now.'

'No, no. You're alright,' said Jack. 'Ignore him. He just gets nervous around the police, that's all.'

'And why's that?'

'I've no idea,' said Jack. 'Maybe it's a fear of authority.'

'Or maybe it's guilt,' said West. 'So, back to these fishing trips of yours, do you always hire McClusky's boat, the *Thistledonia*?'

'Aye, but not now. Not anymore. We've had it with him.'

'How so?' said Duncan. 'Have you two fallen out?'

'In a manner of speaking, aye. The whole trip was a waste of time.'

'And why's that?' said West. 'Was that down to the weather, or because you didn't catch anything?'

Jack glanced at his brother and hesitated before answering.

'It's because he left us high and dry.'

'McClusky?'

'The skipper.'

'The skipper? I though you two went out on your own?'

Jack's eyes flicked from West to Henry, and back again.

'Don't be daft,' he said. 'We're not sailors. We do the fishing, someone else pilots the boat.'

Duncan, amused by his inability to deliver a convincing off the cuff version of events without a degree of reassurance from his brother, thrust his hands deep into his pockets, stared at Jack, and smiled.

'See here, pal,' he said, 'I'm not being funny, but if you can't answer a question without consulting your brother first, then you and I are going to have to have a wee chat someplace else. Are you with me? So, what's all this about the skipper?'

'He was a pain in the arse,' said Jack. 'Not lazy, just foreign. We couldn't understand a word he said. Not that he said much, anyway.'

'Foreign? Where foreign?'

'No idea. Sweden, I think. Or Norway.'

'And does he have a name?'

'Probably,' said Jack, 'but he never told us. We just called him Erik.'

'Erik?'

'Aye, like, Erik the Viking.'

'And what did he look like?' said West. 'This Erik geezer.'

Jack held a hand to his shoulders and pursed his lips.

'About so high,' he said. 'Dark hair. Beard.'

'So, what happened?'

'We were on the return leg…'

'From where?'

Cringing at Jack's blank expression and the ensuing silence, Henry stepped forward and began coiling the hose.

'Harris,' he said, avoiding eye contact. 'We'd got as far as Harris before turning back.'

'Okay, go on.'

'We'd been going two days and we'd got as far as Arran. It was too late to make it back to Kirkcudbright, so we stopped in Troon for the night.'

'Where did you stay?' said Duncan. 'Not on the boat, obviously?'

'No, no. The Anchorage Hotel. Twin room.'

'Can you prove that?'

'Aye, we've got a receipt and we paid by credit card. You can call them if you like.'

'And the skipper?'

'He took a single, I think,' said Jack. 'Although, I can't actually remember seeing him check in.'

'That's handy,' said West. 'So, you stopped the night and then what? Set off in the morning?'

'Aye. But not on the boat. It was gone.'

'Gone?'

'Aye! Gone! Just gone! He took off without us.'

'So, did you call McClusky?' said West. 'Did you explain what had happened?'

'I did,' said Jack. 'I called him right away but he didn't seem that fussed. He just said to get ourselves home and he'd give us our money back as soon as we saw him.'

'And when was that?'

'Are you joking me? We're not long back ourselves. We'll not get down to Kirkcudbright until tomorrow at least.'

'That must have been a pig of a journey,' said West. 'I mean, apart from the disappointment, having to lug all your gear around. What do you call it? Tackle?'

'We didn't have–'

'What he means,' said Henry, butting in, 'is that we didn't have it with us. It was all on the boat.'

'Well, I hope it's insured,' said Duncan, 'a decent fishing rod's not cheap, is it? Still, at least it means you could sit back and enjoy the train ride, right?'

'Aye, it wasn't too bad,' said Jack, 'all things considered. Only an hour or so.'

'From Troon?'

'Aye.'

'To where?'

'Lockerbie. That's the nearest stop to here. Then it's a bus.'

Duncan glanced at West, took a step sideways, and peered past the brothers at the rear of the car.

'That'll need a jet-wash,' he said, nodding at the tow-bar caked with dirt. 'Your rear end's bogging.'

'We've not got a jet-wash,' said Jack. 'Just plenty of elbow grease.'

'We'll leave you to it, then,' said West. 'Looks like you've got your work cut out for you. We'll be in touch.'

* * *

Believing Jack and Henry Boyd's alibi to be about as watertight as a colander, Duncan sat with his head buried in his phone while West, determined to sample some of Moffat's finest offerings, disappeared down the street only to return a few minutes later with an ice cream cone in one hand and a bag of toffee in the other.

'What's going on?' she said as she slipped behind the wheel.

'You drive,' said Duncan. 'I'm busy.'

'Nice one. So, what do you think? Not the sharpest tools in the shed, are they?'

'Jack and Henry? Oh, they're sharper than you think, miss, just not that clued up on public transport.'

'Elaborate,' said West as she polished off the ice cream.

'I've been doing some checking. If you want to get from Troon to Lockerbie in an hour or so, you'll be needing an ambulance.'

'What do you mean?'

'The average journey time is two and a half hours,' said Duncan, 'and there's no direct service. You have to change at Glasgow Central and maybe again at Carlisle.'

'So, someone's been telling porkies.'

'Aye, and there's something else,' said Duncan. 'Mud. That 4x4's covered in clumps of sticky mud.'

'Ah, now I'm ahead of you there,' said West. 'The mud was wet, which means only one thing. They had that motor out this morning.'

'Aye, but they said they'd only just got back. What do you think? Will we bring them in?'

West, in an uncharacteristic show of patience, thought for a moment and unwrapped a toffee.

'No, not yet,' she said as she fired up the Audi. 'I don't want to jump the gun. Give Dougal a shout, tell him we need a background check on those two johnnies just as soon as he can do it.'

'Roger that,' said Duncan.

'And I want him to check CCTV from Troon and Lockerbie, let's see if we can pick them up either coming or going. We'll nip back to their gaff later, get their prints, and invite them in for a Q&A session.'

'Okey-dokey. So, what now?'

'Let's shoot back to Kirkcudbright. I want to have another word with McClusky about the skipper.'

'You and me both,' said Duncan, wincing as the Audi fishtailed across the street, 'but if you don't slow down, we may not get the chance.'

* * *

Aware of his burgeoning reputation as a surly maverick influenced in no small way by the shenanigans of Frank Serpico and a young DI Munro, Duncan, whilst not averse to over-stepping the mark, was careful just to bend the rules whereas West, as a result of her dogged impetuosity, had a habit of unwittingly snapping them in two.

Speeding past the harbour, she careered along Bridge Street, bumped the kerb, and stopped on a double yellow opposite the betting shop, unaware that she'd violated three traffic regulations in the space of fifteen seconds.

'Not being funny, miss,' he said, 'but apart from a burning desire to land yourself a ticket, is there a reason why we're stopping here?'

'Is your memory going?' said West. 'McClusky! He said he was going to put a bet on.'

'Aye! But that was ages ago!'

'Listen, if there's one thing I've learned from all the losers I've had the misfortune to waste my life with, it's that no-one walks into a bookies and walks straight out again. They sit there waiting for the one win that's going to turn their lives around.'

'Maybe I'll nip in there myself,' said Duncan. 'I might get lucky. No offence, but would it not be easier just to call the fella and find out where he is?'

West turned to Duncan and smiled as she wound down the window.

'Oi!' she said, yelling across the street. 'Any luck?'

McClusky stopped in his tracks, nodded, and wandered over.

'With what?' he said.

'The three-thirty?'

'Those horses came in a couple of hours ago, Inspector. Unfortunately, mine's still running.'

'Never mind,' said West. 'Hop in, we need a word.'

'Is it about my boat?' said McClusky as he squeezed his ample frame into the back seat. 'Have you come to tell me I can have it back?'

'Sorry,' said Duncan, 'like we said before, you'll not be seeing that for a while, yet.'

'Well, what is it, then?'

'The lads who rented your boat; Jack and Henry.'

'Aye?'

'Have you spoken to them recently?'

'Not recently,' said McClusky, 'but I did last night.'

'You didn't mention it earlier,' said West. 'Why not?'

'You didn't ask.'

'Well, I am now. Would you mind telling us what it was about?'

'A spot of bother with the *Thistledonia*. Apparently.'

'What do you mean?'

'The fuel pump,' said McClusky. 'They said the fuel pump was clogged and they'd had to stop for repairs.'

'Do you know where they were?'

'Troon. So they said.'

'And was that it?' said West. 'Did they mention anything else?'

'No. They said they were stopping overnight and they'd be on their way just as soon as it was fixed, but I've not heard from them since.'

'Your boat,' said Duncan, 'does it have a habit of breaking down?'

'Certainly not,' said McClusky. 'She's in first class condition, normally runs as smooth as anything.'

'So, this must have come as a bit of surprise, then?'

'Aye, but these things happen, so it's not worth fretting over.'

'Maybe that's why the boat beached,' said Duncan. 'Maybe they didn't get it fixed after all.'

'I'm not sure about that,' said McClusky. 'If the fuel pump was faulty, she'd not have any power. They'd be at the mercy of the tide.'

'Have you any idea what it might have been, then?' said West. 'If it wasn't the fuel pump?'

'I'm not a psychic, Inspector. Once I get it back, I'll have the mechanic give her the once over. He'll soon find out what the problem was.'

'Okay, just one more thing, Mr McClusky,' said Duncan. 'We need another name.'

'You've lost me,' said McClusky. 'I've already told you, the fellas who took the boat out were Jack and Henry Boyd.'

'Yeah, yeah, we've got that,' said West. 'They took it out as paying guests but what we need is the name of the bloke who went with them. The name of the skipper.'

McClusky cocked his head and frowned.

'Skipper?' he said. 'There was no skipper, Inspector. Just the lads, and not a skipper in sight.'

Chapter 6

With the risk of a relapse hanging over his head, a stoical and fiercely independent Munro, whilst refusing to share his anxieties about convalescing alone, had, under duress, begrudgingly accepted to remain as a house guest under the watchful eye of Charlie West until he was back on his feet, the upside for West being the convivial company of a boarder with a penchant for washing dishes whilst the downside was a self-imposed abstention from cooking anything herby, spicy, or pungent, lest it send his blood pressure crashing through the roof.

With Munro back in his own home, West – no longer constrained by the state of his health nor for that matter his uneducated palate – demolished a large slice of pan-fried garlic steak smothered with onions and, saddened by the lack of a whimsical aside regarding the apartment smelling like a Transylvanian tavern after sundown, poured herself a large glass of red, picked up the phone, and dialled.

'Blimey,' she said, 'you took your time. I didn't wake you, did I?'

'I may be getting on, Charlie, but I'm not in the habit of falling asleep in front of the telly with soup dribbling down my chin. Not just yet, anyway.'

'Give it time,' said West. 'So, come on then, what's going on?'

'Not enough to spark a fire,' said Munro. 'Walking, eating, sleeping. That appears to be my routine just now.'

'Good, you need to take it easy. And how's Murdo?'

'The wee mutt's beside me on the sofa.'

'Begging for food, no doubt?'

'Aye, but unlike yourself, Charlie, he'll not be getting any, not until I've finished watching the local news.'

'I don't know why you bother,' said West, 'it's all doom and gloom.'

'You know me, lassie. I'm not happy unless I'm being miserable.'

'What is it this time? A broken-down tractor on the B14762 or was someone short-changed in the pub?'

'I'll not know unless I watch it.'

'Well, pardon me for interrupting,' said West. 'We were down your way earlier. I was going to drop in but you know how it is, time just flew by.'

'Just a minute,' said Munro, 'what do you mean you were down my way? Dumfries and Galloway is not in your jurisdiction.'

'I know, but we had a fishing boat wash up near Girvan and the owner lives in Kirkcudbright.'

Irritated by West's reluctance to divulge any detail, Munro paused for a large sip of Balvenie.

'Let's have it,' he said, sternly. 'I'm all ears.'

'What do you mean?'

'Och, I'm not stupid, lassie. If it was just a wee boat on the beach then uniform could have handled it. What's the story?'

'Well, as you ask, we found something in the hold and we think it's Scandinavian.'

'You're not talking flat-pack furniture, are you?'

'Nope, and it wasn't fish either, although come to think of it, the poor bugger had been filleted. The funny thing is, there was no-one else on the boat.'

'I see. And this boat, was it damaged in any way? A hole in the hull, perhaps?'

'Not that we could see.'

'And the weather?'

'A bit breezy, but even I've been out in worse.'

'And the emergency beacon, had it been activated?'

'What beacon?'

'For heaven's sake, Charlie! Were there not any spent flares on deck? Or any flags flying?'

'Flags? Give me a break, Jimbo! For Christ's sake, I haven't got a clue what you're talking about! Who do you think I am? Ellen bleeding MacArthur?'

'It sounds to me as if–'

'Now hold on,' said West, 'don't you go getting any ideas about packing a bag and heading up here, you need to relax!'

'I was about to say, it sounds to me as if you need to contact the MAIB.'

'Oh. We have. I'll get their findings in the morning.'

'And is that as far as you've got?'

'Give me some credit,' said West. 'We've already met the two geezers who chartered the boat, and we've got their prints, so we're ahead of the game.'

'Forgive me, Charlie,' said Munro, 'but how did you manage that? Have you arrested them?'

'Not yet.'

'Then how did you get their prints?'

'Mobile scanner,' said West. 'This is the twenty-first century, Jimbo. You should get one, they're all the rage.'

'Och, I'm not one for progress, lassie. Give me an ink pad and a sheet of paper any day.'

'They're attending voluntarily tomorrow.'

'And you're sure they'll arrive?'

'Well, if they don't,' said West, 'then I will nick them.'

'On what grounds?'

'Suspicion of murder, of course. Frankly, Jimbo, their story's like a lump of Swiss cheese, besides, they were the last two people known to be on the boat.'

'Are you not hedging your bets, Charlie? If you've nothing to place them at the scene, then it sounds to me as if you're going out on a limb, here.'

'Maybe, but it's a chance I'm willing to take. The bottom line is, if I do arrest them, and they're not guilty, we let them go, no harm done. Duncan's going to question them tomorrow, and while he's doing that, SOCOs will be giving their place the once over.'

'Perhaps age is playing tricks with my cognitive ability,' said Munro, 'but am I missing something here? If they were on the boat, why is their house of such interest?'

'Simple,' said West. 'They said they travelled from Troon to Lockerbie by train but when we met them, they were washing down a 4x4, and they were in a bit of hurry.'

'And that's important, why?'

'Because if they'd been at sea for nearly two weeks, and then taken the train home, the motor wouldn't have been covered in wet mud.'

'Very good, Charlie. I'm impressed. And what of the owner? Have you found the gentleman who actually owns this boat?'

'Yeah, that was the easy part. Nice bloke, personable enough. He's about the same age as you, a bit younger maybe. Name of McClusky.'

Munro reached for the remote, turned off the television, and took another sip of whisky.

'McClusky?' he said. 'Would that be a Thomas McClusky?'

'Yeah, why? Have you heard of him?'

'It's probably not the same chap,' said Munro, 'but there was a fellow by that name, some years ago now, long before I met you.'

'How long?'

'Och, eleven, twelve years, maybe.'

'You mean he's got form?'

'If it's the same gentleman,' said Munro, 'then definitely, aye. It was all over papers. He was convicted of armed robbery. He and his cronies held up a Loomis van as it went to restock the ATM at the Clydesdale in the town centre.'

'Ah, the good old days,' said West, 'nothing like a bit of smash and grab, it's all cybercrime these days. So, how were they caught?'

'They were victims of their own stupidity,' said Munro. 'A failure to secrete the vehicle in a manner adequate enough to avoid detection, and a proliferation of SmartWater about their persons. McClusky and his three accomplices all went down for nine years apiece but they were out in four.'

'Well, I doubt it's the same McClusky,' said West, 'that would be too much of a coincidence, besides, my one can't walk more than ten yards without getting out of breath. I can hardly see him running around with a shotgun in his hands.'

'So, he's a big chap?'

'Put it this way,' said West, 'if Scotland had a sumo wrestling team, he'd be their captain.'

'He may have piled on the beef since he got out.'

'I think you're chasing your tail, Jimbo. I mean, come on, what are the chances of it being the same bloke? Really?'

Munro leaned back, closed his eyes, and frowned as he conjured up an image of McClusky in his mind.

'Tell me, Charlie,' he said, softly, 'does this fellow look as though somebody used his nose as a dartboard?'

A wry smile crept across his face as West fell silent.

'And his ears, Charlie. Do his ears look as though they came from a vegetable stall?'

'Sometimes,' said West, with a disgruntled sigh, 'I just wish I'd kept my bleeding mouth shut.'

'Well?'

'Alright, alright! So, it sounds like the same bloke but that doesn't mean he's guilty of anything now, I mean he was, what's the word… *nice*. He was just too *nice*.'

'Well, he could've turned a corner,' said Munro, 'I'll grant you that. On the other hand, perhaps he's found God. Aye, I can see him now, offering up his spare time for free, giving under-privileged members of society a sail around the harbour.'

'Get to the point.'

'Two words, Charlie: leopard, and spots.'

* * *

With a diary devoid of social engagements and a husband who preferred to fraternise with his flock rather than mingle with the neighbours, Maureen Baxter had long since regarded the task of pressing her own clothes as nothing more than an exercise in futility.

Bundling her blouses, skirts, and slacks into a laundry basket, she glanced out of the window and, with the night as black as pitch and still no sign of her husband, poured herself three fingers of her favourite malt and set about collecting another load for the washing machine, when the faint sound of a car easing up the drive drew her to the hall.

Drained by the strain of spending the entire afternoon hunched over the wheel of his pick-up scouring the verges and the hedgerows of the coastal road for any sign of his daughter, a weary Willy Baxter, having taken a full three hours to cover twenty-five miles, groaned as he stepped through the door.

'At least it's not raining,' he said, rubbing his eyes with the backs of his hands, 'that's something to be grateful for.'

'Oh, it's yourself,' said Maureen, 'I was starting to worry. Where have you been?'

'Everywhere,' said Baxter. 'First, I went for a walk up the woods, and I even checked the old bothy, just in case she'd decided to have a wee lie-down. Then I drove all the way up to Glendoune and as I was up that way, I called in at the minicab office, I thought, you never know, they might have–'

'And had they?'

'No. They had not. Then after that I went back on myself, all the way down to the pub in Ballantrae. I could have murdered a pint, I'll tell you that for nothing.'

'And?'

'And nothing,' said Baxter. 'I hate to say it, but no-one's seen hide nor hair of the girl.'

'That Rhona,' said Maureen, 'with all this worry she'll have me in my box in no time.'

'Don't be waiting on Rhona, hen. I've a hammer and nails if you're in a hurry. Did you call that Callum fella?'

'I did, aye, but there was no answer. I left a message.'

'Well, maybe he'll call you back,' said Baxter. 'Right, I need to eat, is there any food on the go?'

'Aye, your supper's in the oven,' said Maureen. 'You'll have to help yourself.'

'Oh, aye? And what are you up to?'

'I'm busy washing, then I'm away to tidy the cellar.'

'It's not a cellar!' said Baxter. 'Besides, there's nothing to tidy down there, it's as clean as a whistle.'

'That's as maybe,' said Maureen, 'but that duvet and the pillow won't find their way to the airing cupboard on their own.'

* * *

Alone in the den, she sat for a moment savouring the stone-cold silence and, wishing she'd brought the Glenfiddich with her, began to appreciate why the room, with its rows of books, worn wingback chair, and soft glow of an ageing standard lamp, was such an attraction.

Hit by a wave of apathy at the thought of traipsing back upstairs with nothing to look forward to but a sink full of dirty dishes, she opened the ottoman, tossed the pillow inside and crammed the duvet on top, confounded by the feel of something substantially firmer than a layer of duck down tucked within its folds.

'Willy Baxter!' she said, yelling at the top of her voice. 'You need to come here, this minute!'

Baxter, a bowl in one hand and a napkin in the other, ambled down the stairs to find his wife perched on the edge of the sofa with the contents of a handbag scattered beside her.

'What is it, woman?' he said, as he took a mouthful of crumble. 'It's not a mouse, is it?'

Maureen, her face riddled with angst, held a brown, leather tote aloft and frowned.

'It's Rhona's,' she said, 'and look, it's her purse. Where would she go without her purse?'

'Maybe she had some cash in her pockets.'

'No, no. There's money here, and all her cards. And her phone. Willy, look at the phone, it says one missed call. That's my number, from when I called her earlier.'

'She's not had any other calls?'

'None.'

'Any text messages?'

'No. Where on earth has she gone, Willy? Where?'

Baxter set his bowl on the side and wiped his mouth.

'Well,' he said, 'if she's not been hit by lightning, or walked into the sea, then I'm afraid, Maureen, I haven't the foggiest.'

'There's something else.'

Maureen, her hand trembling, passed him a small Jiffy bag and watched his brow furrow in disbelief as he fingered through the bundle of banknotes.

'Am I seeing things?' he said. 'There's hundreds here! A couple of thousand, maybe.'

'Where did she get that kind of money?'

'You don't suppose she was–'

'Willy Baxter! That's our daughter you're talking about!'

'Just asking, hen. The question is, if she has this kind of money, then why did she lose her flat? Why could she not pay her rent?'

'Perhaps it's not hers,' said Maureen. 'Or perhaps it's her–'

'Stop havering, woman! You know as well as I do, something's not right here, not right at all. I'm away to make a telephone call.'

'A call?' said Maureen. 'But who? Who will you phone at this time of night?'

'Who do you think?' said Baxter, as he made his way upstairs. 'I'm calling the police.

Chapter 7

Despite a commendably courageous but ultimately doomed attempt at changing his image from that of a bookish intellectual to an alpha male capable of terrifying the most hardened of criminals, the mild-mannered DS Dougal McCrae, having fallen at the first hurdle, remained haunted by his reputation for being socially inept which was compounded by an irrational fear of the opposite sex.

With just one relationship in three years – a dalliance which comprised a handful of dates with a law graduate whose insatiable libido had left him on the verge of a nervous breakdown – having to sit uncomfortably close to the mousey yet undeniably attractive Kay Grogan, a young scenes of crime officer who not only shared his love of criminology but harboured a passion for freshwater fishing too, had him quaking in his boots.

'Alright?' said West as she breezed through the door. 'Blimey, a full house! Who's this then?'

Dougal, his cheeks flushing, peered at West from behind his computer screen.

'This is Kay,' he said sheepishly. 'I mean, Miss Grogan. Kay Grogan. She's a SOCO.'

'How's it going?' said West. 'It's not often we see your sort in here, especially this early.'

'Oh, we've not been to bed,' said Grogan. 'We've been up all night on the *Thistledonia*.'

West placed a brown paper carrier bag on the desk, raised her eyebrows, and smiled.

'I have to say, you're looking surprisingly fresh for someone who's been up all night. That goes for you, too, Dougal. Something must be charging your batteries.'

'Aye,' said Duncan with a grin, 'no prizes for guessing what that is!'

'Well, you must be starving,' said West. 'Here we go, two square sausage, two bacon, and two fried egg. Take your pick.'

'You're alright,' said Dougal. 'Thanks all the same, miss, but we've already had ours.'

'Oh, very cosy, I must say!'

'I'll take his,' said Duncan, 'I'm needing a full belly before I tackle those two numpties. They're here already.'

'Well, in that case,' said West, wiring into a bacon roll, 'we'd better get a wiggle on. It looks like you've been busy, so, have we got anywhere yet?'

'We're steaming ahead,' said Duncan. 'I'll go first, you can chat with Dougal and the delightful Miss Grogan while I'm away.'

'Okay, shoot.'

'Background checks–'

'Hold on!' said West. 'Sorry to interrupt, but that reminds me. Dougal, we need a background check on Tam McClusky, and dig deep, he's got previous.'

'Are you joking me?' said Duncan. 'How d'you figure that?'

'I had a word with Jimbo last night. Apparently, he went down for armed robbery a few years ago.'

'Well, he's keeping good company,' said Duncan. 'That Henry Boyd, the younger of the two, he's got form, too.'

'So, his brother was right,' said West. 'He does have a fear of authority after all.'

'Aye, which is why he likes to keep his mouth shut.'

'So, what's the score?'

'Aggravated assault,' said Duncan, 'and it's recent, too. Nine months back, he's on a suspended. He claimed some fella tried to mug him for his bag and he was only acting in self-defence but CCTV shows him pulverising the alleged thief beyond all recognition.'

'So why didn't he go down?'

'The judge accepted his brief's defence of "an uncharacteristic moment of madness" due to stress and fatigue. That, and an unblemished record, got him off.'

'Do we know who tried to snatch his bag?'

'Some chancer who'd been doing the rounds of all the pubs in the area.'

'Get a name. You never know, it might come in handy. What about his brother Jack? Has he had his collar felt?'

'No,' said Duncan, 'officially, he's clean.'

'What do you mean, officially?'

Duncan glanced at West, scratched the stubble on his chin, and offered up a roguish smile.

'I mean, he's not been in trouble,' he said, 'not yet. However, I've just been looking into their company's activities.'

'And?'

'Okay, get this. He and his brother, as you know, they're a couple of jobbing builders, handymen, if you will. Now, they've got a limited company, they call themselves "Moffat Repair and Restoration", and that Jack, he's a good lad, I'll give him that. He's filed their returns on time, every year, for the past four years.'

'It seems like it's all above board,' said West. 'So, what's the problem?'

'The problem I'm having, miss, is how do a couple of labourers manage a turnover of five hundred and fifty thousand pounds–'

'Are you having a laugh?'

'–and yet, after salaries and allowable expenses, make a loss of nine hundred and sixty-two pounds?'

West stared at Duncan, dusted off her fingers, and reached for another roll.

'Sounds to me like they're running a laundry service.'

'Aye, that's what I thought, so I've asked HMRC to send us a copy of their latest return.'

'Nice one,' said West. 'So, what's next? Apart from a decent cuppa.'

'Not for me,' said Duncan, 'I'm away downstairs. Dougal, have we enough to hold them?'

'Oh, aye, Jack Boyd, definitely. Two counts, at least.'

'Text me the details. Miss, I'll leave you in the capable hands of Dougal and his lady friend. I mean, colleague.'

West filled the kettle, returned to her seat, and smiled at Grogan.

'So, what happened, Kay?' she said, with a wink. 'Did you draw the short straw?'

'Sorry, Inspector? I'm not sure I'm with you.'

'Getting lumbered with Dougal, here.'

'Oh, no, I offered! I thought, as this was a matter of some urgency, it was probably best if we ran through my findings now. Together. I can send a written report over later.'

'Well, I hate to pile on the pressure,' said West, 'especially after an all-nighter, but Dougal, don't forget we've got SOCOs heading over to the Boyds' place later. You need to be there.'

'Oh, that's me,' said Grogan. 'Dougal's going to run me down there on his scooter.'

'Is he, by George?'

'Aye, well, normally I'd not bother,' said Grogan, 'I'd arrange for somebody else to fill-in for me, but Dougal's smashing to work with.'

'Isn't he just?'

'Aye. Did you know he's into fishing, too?'

'Is he really?' said West, sarcastically. 'You mean you're–?'

'Oh, aye, it's the best. The problem is, the only fellas I ever meet are either past it, or they spend their entire day sitting on the bank supping ale from a six-pack.'

'I take it you're not much of a drinker, then?'

'No. A wee lager now and then, that's all. I'm a pescatarian, too.'

'Well, Dougal's a Virgo so you should get on well. Right, what have you got for me?'

Grogan spun on her seat, pulled a notebook from her bag, and glanced coyly at Dougal as she flicked to the relevant page.

'Let's start with the weapon,' she said, 'the knife that was lying beside the body.'

'Go on.'

'The good news is, being below deck with the hatch closed, it was protected from the elements.'

'But?'

'But I'm afraid there's no prints, and of course, we shall have to wait for Dr McLeod to confirm that it is actually the murder weapon, but having said that, the FLS did pick up plenty of body fluid on the blade, and that can only have come from the victim. We also found a few other bits and bobs, the usual fibres and such. I doubt they'll amount to much but they're away for testing anyway.'

'Well, disappointing about the prints,' said West, 'but it's a start.'

'Don't be too disheartened, Inspector,' said Grogan. 'I did manage to get some prints from the wheelhouse.'

'Blinding! And they obviously match the victim?'

'I'm afraid not.'

'What?'

'They're not his,' said Grogan, 'but we did get a match.'

'You're going to love this,' said Dougal. 'It's Jack Boyd.'

'You are kidding?'

'No, no. We already had his prints, miss. All it took was a wee look on the system, it's a perfect match.'

'And you're absolutely sure?'

'One hundred per cent. Kay got some cracking samples off the screen on the chartplotter. It's definitely him.'

West, requesting a pause in proceedings, raised her hand as she returned to the kitchen, filled the mugs, and pondered the implications.

'The things is,' she said, 'Jack Boyd swears blind that neither he nor his brother know the first thing about sailing a boat, so why would his dabs be on that piece of equipment?'

'Oh, it's not just the plotter,' said Grogan, 'we found his prints all over the bridge, and on the inside of the door as well.'

'There's something else,' said Dougal, 'something Kay found on the floor.'

'Well, don't keep me in suspense,' said West. 'What is it?'

'Boot prints,' said Grogan. 'A set of latent boot prints. Rubber sole, relatively new. There's hardly any sign of wear on the heel or toe.'

'Is there anything distinctive about them? Anything that'll make identifying the wearer easier for us?'

'Not really,' said Grogan, 'but they do have a chevron-style tread and I believe that to be unique to one manufacturer.'

'Go on?'

'Dunlop, but don't get your hopes up, they're one of the most popular brands around.'

'Okay, well, regardless of who makes them, please tell me they belong to the bloke in the hold.'

Grogan smiled apologetically and shook her head.

'The victim takes an eight,' she said. 'The prints in the cabin are a ten. Could they belong to one of yourselves, maybe?'

'No, no,' said Dougal, 'we were all wearing boot socks when we went aboard.'

'Then it must be one of the Boyd fellas.'

'Dougal, whizz downstairs,' said West, 'not now, later, find out what size boot they take. Kay, what about the deck? I mean, McLeod seems to think that that's where the bugger was sliced open.'

'Aye, I'll not contest that,' said Grogan, 'but what with the rain and the sea-spray, there's nothing, I'm afraid.'

West swung her feet onto the desk, sipped her tea, and stared pensively into space.

'I'm not keen on liars,' she said, 'and it seems to me that those two boys have been telling porkies from day one. Give me a second while I buzz Duncan, he could do with this info.'

'Hang fire,' said Dougal. 'You may as well load both barrels before you text him.'

'Alright then, off you go.'

'We found an EPIRB in a cupboard on the bridge–'

'English, please!'

'Sorry. An Emergency Position-Indicating Radio Beacon.'

'So, that's what Jimbo was talking about! Explain, and keep it simple.'

'Okay, there's two types,' said Dougal. 'There's the kind which crew carry about their persons, about the size of a mobile phone, and the bigger ones which are kept on the boat. Both devices are GPS enabled and once activated emit a signal once every forty-five seconds or thereabouts, so anyone in distress can be located by the emergency services or even any passing vessels.'

'Don't tell me.'

'Correct. This one had not been activated, which leads me to believe–'

'That there wasn't an accident after all,' said West. 'That they were in complete control of the boat before it beached.'

'Exactly,' said Dougal. 'And that theory has been substantiated by the MAIB's assessment of the *Thistledonia.* According to them she was perfectly sea-worthy and in good, working order but–'

'Go on.'

'–the throttle had left been left open and, with no crew aboard, they've concluded that she was probably scuppered deliberately.'

West, hankering after the days when a murder victim would be found flat on his back outside a chicken shop with a machete wedged in his neck, and the perp had the decency to stare directly into the lens of a security camera, stood up, slipped her hands into her pockets, and wandered slowly round the desk.

'Could this be some kind of insurance scam?' she said. 'I mean, forget about the bloke in the hold for a minute, could they claim the accident on adverse weather conditions and pocket a few grand?'

'Absolutely not,' said Dougal. 'I've already checked with the Maritime and Coastguard Agency for the six hours leading up to the accident. Conditions for Hebrides and Malin were wind – southwest two to three – rain, then showers, visibility good to moderate. An eight-year-old in a paper boat could have sailed in those conditions.'

'Okay, then help me out here, Dougal. We all think, that is, you, me, and the MAIB, that the boat was run aground on purpose.'

'Undoubtedly, miss.'

'So, tell me, is that an offence of any sort?'

'Oh, aye!' said Dougal. 'Under the Merchant Shipping Act, it most certainly is. Whoever was at the helm could be hit with a hefty fine or even a custodial plus, a failure to report the incident to the MAIB would carry further penalties.'

'So, at the very least,' said West, 'if we can prove that Jack Boyd was in charge of the vessel at the time of the crash, we could do him for that?'

'Right enough.'

A befuddled-looking Grogan leaned back, folded her arms, and stared inquisitively at West.

'You alright?' said West. 'What's up?'

'Sorry, I know it's not my place to interfere, Inspector, but it doesn't make sense to me. I mean, why run the boat aground? If they wanted to get rid of the body, could they not have tossed it overboard? Or even torched the boat, maybe?'

'Good question,' said West. 'I'll let Dougal answer that one.'

'Well, for start,' said Dougal, 'if they'd lobbed the body overboard, chances are it would have washed up within an hour or two, and if they'd set the boat alight, blues and twos would have been there in a matter of minutes.'

'Yeah, but we found him anyway,' said West. 'So, what difference would that have made?'

'Time. Time for a getaway. Either that, or they wanted us to find him.'

'And why would they want us to do that? We don't even know who the poor sod is.'

'We do now,' said Dougal, grinning as he waved a wallet in the air. 'In here is a driving licence and a couple of bank cards, and guess what, miss? He's not Scandinavian at all. He's an Icelandic national, name of Aron Jónsson. Forty-two years old, and he lives in Höfn.'

'Iceland?' said West. 'Blimey, he's a bit far from home, isn't he? Have you contacted the embassy in London, yet?'

'Miss, I've just the one pair of hands. I'll do it later.'

'Fair enough. Carry on, this is finally getting interesting.'

'Okey-dokey. This is a wee bit techy, so don't get the hump if you don't understand.'

'As if I would.'

'I've downloaded all the data from the chartplotter and the AIS.'

'Remind me.'

'The Automatic Identification System.'

'Of course it is.'

'In basic terms, it monitors traffic in the area,' said Dougal, 'collision avoidance, if you will, and if the other boats are properly registered, it'll identify them, too.'

'Okay, I'm with you so far.'

'According to the chartplotter,' said Dougal, 'the Boyds were en route for–'

'Don't tell me! Harris!'

'You're heading in the right direction, but you're wide of the mark. Very wide. They'd plotted a course for the Faroe Islands.'

'Where the flipping heck are the Faroe Islands?'

'North of Scotland, miss, slap bang in the middle between Iceland and Norway, but they never got there.'

'I'm not surprised,' said West, 'surely you'd need the QEII to get up there. What happened?'

'According to the AIS, they stopped in the Outer Hebrides, near St Kilda to be precise, and get this, it looks as though they might have been met by another ship called the *Loki*.'

'Loki? What's Loki?'

'In Norse mythology, he's the god of fire, and a wee bit of a mischief-maker.'

'You never cease to amaze me,' said West. 'You're a mind of useless information, you are.'

'I can't take all the credit, miss. Wikipedia helped me out.'

'I admire your honesty, but where's all this leading us?'

'The *Loki*,' said Dougal, 'is an Icelandic vessel. A stern trawler, registration VE117. It was close by, I mean, really close. It's impossible to be one hundred per cent accurate but it does look as though both boats stopped for a while, ten or fifteen minutes maybe, before the *Thistledonia* headed back south.'

West, beginning to wonder if she was due any sick leave, ruffled her hair and gazed at Dougal with a look of bewilderment.

'Tell me if I'm missing something,' she said, 'because I don't know one end of a rod from the other, but isn't that a bit far to go just to catch a few fish?'

'It is,' said Dougal, 'especially as they were line-fishing. They could have been after lobster or shrimp, but they'd have needed a creel for any of the pelagic species.'

'If you say so. Okay, so as far as we know, the skipper, otherwise known as the dead bloke in the hold, was Icelandic. And Jack and Henry Boyd sailed off to meet a boat in the middle of nowhere, which was also Icelandic.'

'Maybe,' said Dougal, 'but we don't know for sure. It's possible the Boyds saw the size of the *Loki*, realised they'd bitten off more than they could chew, and simply turned back.'

'Oh, this is smashing!' said Grogan. 'I never get to see you fellas working close-up like this. It's like watching one of those shows on the telly.'

'Trust me,' said West, 'it's nothing like the flipping telly. It's all insomnia and headache pills washed down with a gallon of grief. So, is that it, then? Is this the end of the road?'

Dougal glanced at Grogan and raised a subtle smile like a gambler about to reveal his winning hand.

'Not quite,' he said. 'We know the *Thistledonia* docked in Troon, okay? And from there, according to the chartplotter, it was on a course for Kirkcudbright, but as we also know, she never made it.'

'Oh, state the bleeding obvious, why don't you!' said West. 'Of course she never made it, she ran aground!'

'Right enough,' said Dougal, 'but just before that, she stopped for a second time, the co-ordinates were 55.1681° north, and 4.9361° west, which is roughly half a nautical mile off the coast of Lendalfoot.'

'Why?'

'If I knew that, miss, I'd not be sitting here, but perhaps that's where the crew abandoned ship.'

'What about that sat nav thing,' said West, 'did it pick up any other boats when it stopped?'

'None that we know of, but they could have been met by a wee pleasure craft, or maybe they even swam ashore.'

'Swam ashore? Are you serious?'

'They'd have been carried by the tide,' said Dougal, 'and if they wore a wetsuit, then it's not out of the realms of possibility.'

'I might try it myself,' said West, 'with a couple of bricks tied to my legs.'

'Well, while you're at the builders merchants fetching some rope, I'll run Kay back to the office.'

'Don't forget to check on McClusky,' said West, reaching for her phone. 'I'm going to give Duncan a bell.'

***

Faced with a choice of interrupting his interview with a phone call or running downstairs to update him in person, West, filching a slice of sausage from one of the remaining rolls, opted to savour the serenity of the empty office instead and began composing a lengthy text message when the unexpected arrival of the ebullient DCI Elliot had her jumping in her seat.

'Charlie!' he said, his voice booming like a tenor in the opera house. 'On your lonesome?'

'Sir. You've just missed them. Duncan's with a suspect and Dougal's… on an errand.'

'No bother! It's you I came to see.'

'Nothing serious, I hope?'

'If it was, Charlie, we'd not be here, we'd be in my office! See here, the gentleman who found the boat you're looking into, he goes by the name of Baxter, does he not?'

'Spot on,' said West. 'Willy Baxter, why? What's up?'

'Uniform are in attendance now, apparently his daughter's gone missing. I thought you might want to follow up, that's all.'

Chapter 8

Unlike his younger brother who'd forsaken an education in favour of fraternising with the scallies and lowlifes loafing about the penurious streets of Dumfries, Jack Boyd, whilst lacking the sagacity to complete a crossword, was nonetheless blessed with a brain attuned to the art of cunning and deception. It was a talent which had, through years of orchestrating a string of petty but lucrative deals in the pubs and clubs of Lochside, brought him enough untraceable wealth to acquire a house in the picturesque town of Moffat where, behind the guise of a successful company, he'd continued to ply his trade as a purveyor of illegally sourced tobacco, alcohol, and the occasional BMW, completely undetected.

Unfazed by the surroundings of the interview room, he sat with the relaxed demeanour of a koala on ketamine while Duncan, smiling smugly to himself, scrolled through a message on his phone.

'Sorry about that,' he said, stabbing the voice recorder. 'Just some business to attend to.'

'No bother,' said Boyd. 'Is my brother not coming?'

'No, no. I'll have a chat with him after. Now, can I get you anything to drink? A tea, or a coffee, maybe?'

'You're alright,' said Boyd. 'If it's all the same with you I'd rather crack on so's I can get back to work.'

'Are you busy, then?'

'Aye, busy enough. It doesn't help having to come all the way up here. Could we not have done this in Dumfy?'

'Afraid not,' said Duncan, 'but you are here voluntarily, so you're welcome to leave any time you like.'

'Aye, okay.'

'And you're entitled to legal representation, if you want it.'

'Do I need it?' said Boyd. 'I mean, you're not arresting me, are you?'

'No, not yet,' said Duncan with a wry smile, 'but you never know your luck.'

'Then I'll not bother.'

'Okay. For the benefit of the tape, I am Detective Sergeant Reid. Would you state your name, please.'

'Jack Boyd.'

'Do you understand why you're here, Jack?'

'Not really, no.'

'Two reasons,' said Duncan. 'First of all, we've found the boat that you chartered, the *Thistledonia*. She was beached a couple of miles south of Girvan.'

'I'm not surprised,' said Boyd, 'like I said yesterday, Erik the Viking's probably the worst skipper we've ever had.'

'What makes you think he was on the boat?'

'Well, who else would have taken it?'

'Fair point.'

'So, what's the second reason?' said Boyd. 'You said there were two reasons for me being here.'

'Right enough,' said Duncan. 'I'm afraid your recollection of events has left us a wee bit confused so I just need to clarify a few points. Are you okay with that?'

'No bother. Fire away and I'll see what I can do.'

'Good. So, what time was it when we arrived at your place yesterday? About one-thirty, is that right?'

'I'd say so, aye.'

'And you'd just got back yourselves. Do you remember when that was, exactly?'

'About twenty minutes before you arrived. A half an hour, maybe.'

'Okay, and you say it took an hour or so for you to travel from Troon back to Moffat?'

'No,' said Boyd, 'I said it took an hour to Lockerbie, then the bus.'

'My mistake. So, in that case, you must have left Troon, when? About eleven-thirty, twelve? Does that sound right?'

'Aye.'

'And the train, was it a direct service, or did you have to change?'

'No, straight through,' said Boyd. 'Is there a problem with that?'

'Aye, there is,' said Duncan. 'You see, Jack, we've checked the timetables and there is no direct service from Troon to Lockerbie. You'd have had to change at least once, and the journey time's two and a half hours, at least.'

Boyd stared at Duncan, leaned forward in his seat, and pushed his spectacles to the bridge of his nose with his middle finger.

'Okay,' he said, 'how's this? Maybe we did change, and I forgot, and maybe I was that tired, I fell asleep, so it seemed like an hour.'

'Aye, that'll be it,' said Duncan, 'I'll check with Henry later but I have to say, I do find it surprising that someone like yourself can get those details so wrong.'

'How so?'

'Well, you've a head on your shoulders, Jack, you're a smart fella, and you're obviously good with figures if you're doing all those tax returns by yourself.'

'Oh, it's not as difficult as they make out,' said Boyd. 'It's the accountants who make it sound complicated so they can earn a few quid. If they came clean, they'd be out of a job.'

'I wouldn't know,' said Duncan, 'being salaried, it's not a problem I have to deal with. Your business, building and restoration, is it?'

'Aye, all sorts,' said Boyd. 'Building, roofing, driveways, you name it, we can probably do it.'

'And would you say it's lucrative?'

'Aye, not bad. It keeps us in clover.'

'I'm sure it does,' said Duncan, 'it must do, with a turnover like yours.'

'I'm not with you.'

'A half a million.'

Boyd smiled and shook his head.

'See here, Sergeant,' he said, 'this is precisely what I'm talking about. This is precisely why accountants make such a good living. You're confusing turnover with profit. If you must know, we actually made a loss last year.'

'How so?'

'Necessary expenditure to keep the business afloat.'

'I see.'

'I know what I'm doing,' said Boyd. 'It's all legit. Take a look yourself if you don't believe me.'

'I will,' said Duncan. 'In fact, I've already had a word with HMRC.'

'Good for you.'

Unimpressed by Boyd's deceptively cool, if not over-confident attitude, a trait he knew to be synonymous with cocky criminal minds, Duncan crossed his arms and proffered a half-hearted smile.

'You've not been in trouble before, have you, Jack?'

'With the law?' said Boyd. 'Not me. Never.'

'I'm wondering, is that because you play by the rules, or because you're good at covering your tracks?'

'I'm a law-abiding citizen, me. I do everything by the book.'

'Unlike your brother.'

‘Well, he’s not as smart as myself,’ said Boyd, ‘but he knows how to look after himself, I’ll give him that.’

‘So I hear. He’s still on a suspended sentence, is he not?’

‘He is, aye.’

‘And what did he do to get a slap on the wrist?’

‘You obviously know.’

‘I do,’ said Duncan, ‘but I’m asking you.’

‘He walloped some chancer in the pub.’

‘Which pub?’

‘Mulligans. It’s not there now. The place was a dive.’

‘And he was out for a few bevvies with a pal, is that it?’

‘He was meeting a client,’ said Boyd. ‘A prospective client. The fella was after a quote on a job.’

‘Is that not a wee bit unusual? I mean, would you not normally go to their house?’

‘He wanted to meet in the pub. He’s the client, he calls the shots.’

‘So, you like to give the personal touch?’

‘It’s a people business,’ said Boyd. ‘We’ve a reputation that’s grown by word of mouth, no advertising, no discounts, just quality work at a decent price.’

‘Good for you,’ said Duncan. ‘So, this chancer, he saw Henry’s bag and he thought he’d try his luck, is that it?’

‘I wasn’t there, but pretty much, aye.’

‘What kind of a bag was it? A plastic carrier from the supermarket? A holdall?’

‘A rucksack.’

‘And what was in it?’

‘Work stuff,’ said Boyd. ‘A few tools, a notebook, that kind of thing.’

‘Then why did Henry go off on one? I mean, for a few wee bits and bobs, he fair beat the fella half to death.’

‘Henry’s funny like that. He lives by his principles; thou shall not steal, and all that.’

‘I’m reminded of one myself,’ said Duncan. ‘Honour amongst thieves. Let’s get back to your fishing trip. You said you always hire a skipper when you charter the boat, and that's because you know nothing about sailing, is that right?'

'Aye, haven't a scooby.'

'And Henry?'

'He can handle a pedalo, but that's about it.'

'So, unless it was honking down or blowing a gale,' said Duncan, 'you'd have no reason to be in the wheelhouse?'

'None that I can think of.'

'Then can you explain why your fingerprints are all over the cabin?'

Boyd, completely unruffled by the question, raised a hand to his chin and gazed pensively at the ceiling.

'It was raining,' he said, 'not hard, just a wee drizzle as we rounded Arran. We may have stepped inside for a while.'

'May have?'

'Aye.'

'And while you were inside,' said Duncan, 'would you have had cause to handle anything? Move things around?'

'No, I told you, that's why we have a skipper.'

'I must be missing something, then,' said Duncan, 'because we found your prints all over a couple of wee computers sitting by the helm.'

'Oh that,' said Boyd. 'I had to move the CP and the AIS so's I had somewhere to sit.'

Duncan leaned across the desk, cocked his head, and frowned.

'Sorry, Jack,' he said, 'you've lost me. The CP?'

'The chartplotter,' said Boyd, 'and the Automatic Identification System. You'll not get far without them.'

'I'm impressed,' said Duncan, his voice tinged with sarcasm, 'but hold on there, I thought you knew nothing about piloting a boat.'

Boyd, for the first time in an otherwise flawless performance, dropped his guard and glanced furtively about the room.

'I don't,' he said, bluntly. 'It's just words, you pick up the terminology when you're surrounded by it.'

'Aye, of course you do,' said Duncan. 'Now, about the skipper. Incidentally, his name's Aron Jónsson by the way and get this, he's not a Viking after all, he's from Iceland.'

'I'm made up for him.'

'Okay, so you're convinced Aron Jónsson took the boat while you and Henry were asleep in your pit, is that right?'

'Who else would've taken it?' said Boyd. 'Not some ned, that's for sure. It's not a Subaru, Sergeant, it's a clapped-out, old fishing boat.'

'Did you not think to ask at the hotel if he'd checked out?'

'What good would that have done?'

'Well, did you not think to call him on his mobile?'

'We didn't have his number,' said Boyd. 'Why would we? We were with him twenty-four hours a day, seven days a week.'

'Good answer. But would it not have made sense to call the police?'

'We called McClusky,' said Boyd. 'We did everything we could.'

'Unfortunately,' said Duncan, 'I'm not convinced you did. See here, Jack, I'll tell you what I think. I think your story about getting the train back to Lockerbie is a complete pack of lies.'

'Oh, aye? And how do you figure that?'

'A wee thing called CCTV. You're not on it. See here, Jack, I think you and Henry sailed the *Thistledonia* from Troon by yourselves. And I think you and Henry scuppered her deliberately off the coast of Lendalfoot.'

'That's quite a story,' said Boyd, 'but tell me this, even if we were on the boat, why would we want to scupper it?'

'Because you couldn't get rid of your passenger.'

'Passenger?'

'The skipper.'

Duncan paused as Boyd's vacuous stare was interrupted by a tell-tale blink.

'There's something else, Jack,' he said, lowering his voice. 'I think you and your brother were also responsible for the attack on Aron Jónsson.'

Boyd hesitated for a moment, swallowed hard, then threw his head back and laughed theatrically.

'You're clutching at straws, now!' he said, his shoulders twitching with mirth. 'I mean, why exactly would we want to kill Aron Jónsson?'

Quietly elated by Boyd's slip of the tongue, Duncan slowly stood, tucked his chair beneath the desk, and smiled.

'Who said he was dead? In fact, Jack, how would you even know he was still on the boat?'

Enveloped by a deafening silence, Boyd cleared his throat, shook his head, and sighed despondently.

'I can see I'm wasting my time here,' he said. 'We're all entitled to our opinions, Sergeant, but yours are off the scale, so if we're all done, then that's me away. I've work to do.'

'I hate to break it to you,' said Duncan as he scrolled through his phone, 'but work's going to have to wait. Jack Boyd… bear with me, pal, this is a newbie for me. Oh aye, here we go. Jack Boyd, I'm arresting you on suspicion of violating the Merchant Shipping Distress and Prevention of Collisions Regulations 1996, and section 58 of the Merchant Shipping Act 1995, whereby you did wilfully cause the vessel known as the *Thistledonia* to run aground, and that you did also fail to report said incident to the Maritime Accident Investigation Branch. I believe that keeping you in custody is necessary and proportionate for the purposes of bringing you before a court where charges will be brought by the Maritime and Coastguard Agency. Do you understand?'

Boyd, his right foot tapping the floor, folded his arms and stared at Duncan with a supercilious smile smeared across his face.

'No big deal,' he said. 'First, you have prove it, which I don't believe you can, and secondly, even if you do, what's the penalty for wrecking a boat? A wee fine? I can afford that, no problem. It's not as if I'll be going down for life.'

'No, of course not,' said Duncan, 'not for that, anyway. But you will for murder.'

'Are you joking me?'

'Jack Boyd, under section 1 of the Criminal Justice Act I am also arresting you on suspicion of the murder of Aron Jónsson. You are not obliged to say anything but anything you do say will be noted and may be used in evidence. Do you understand?'

Chapter 9

Unlike the beautiful south where a sudden cold snap would render the roads impassable and send the snowflakes scurrying to the supermarket to panic-buy crates of avocados and artisan loaves, the weather in Caledonia, though prone to extremes, was best described as seasonal, with the most dramatic changes in the scenery occurring during the onset of winter when, despite the threat of plummeting temperatures, biting winds, and snow-laden clouds looming on the horizon, life went on as normal.

Cruising along the shore road, West, invigorated by a landscape worthy of an Ansel Adams, slowed to a sedate twenty to marvel at the sight of grey seals resting on the rocks where the stricken *Thistledonia* had lain less than thirty-six hours earlier before turning up the lane to the secluded farmhouse where Willy Baxter, standing beneath the front porch with his hands in his pockets, watched a uniformed officer make his way back to the patrol car.

West hopped from the Defender, flashed her warrant card, and smiled as PC Mark Villiers, disgruntled at having to leave the warmth of the office to listen to the ramblings of what he considered to be an over-protective parent, strode hurriedly towards her.

'Alright?' she said. 'DI West, nice day for it. I thought you'd be long gone by now.'

'So did I,' said Villiers, scowling as he gawped at West wearing nothing but a white, cotton tee shirt beneath her biker jacket. 'Are you not cold?'

'Nah, I'm like an Arctic fox, me.'

'I'm more of a reptile, myself. Are you here about the girl, too?'

'Yeah, something like that. Have you got everything you need?'

'Aye, I'd say so,' said Villiers. 'We'll get her registered as missing then do the usual, you know, door-to-doors, then we'll do a sweep of the area but we can't go far, we don't have the resources.'

'What about her gaff?' said West. 'Have you got an address?'

'Aye, but she lives in Stranraer so we'll have to ask Dumfries and Galloway to take a look.'

'Okay, do me a favour and ask them to have a gander as soon as they can. What about transport? Was she driving?'

'No,' said Villiers, 'she's not got a car, and she's left her gear in the house. Her father seems to think she probably went for a walk and either took a fall or got lost, but I'm not convinced.'

'Oh? Why's that?'

'She's not a wean, miss, and she's not a tourist. She's an adult, and she's a local. I'll not be surprised if she's back with her boyfriend or sleeping off a hangover with her pals.'

* * *

Baxter, unaccustomed as he was to receiving visitors, let alone those in uniform, regarded their brief exchange with a degree of trepidation before acknowledging West with a subtle nod of the head.

'Inspector,' he said, glancing skyward. 'Look at that. It's like living in the shadow of Armageddon. We're in for a soaking this afternoon.'

'Well, the ducks will like it.'

'The ducks are welcome to it,' said Baxter, stifling a yawn. 'They're not the ones with rheumatism.'

'You alright?' said West. 'You look done in.'

'Aye, well, I've not had much sleep–'

'Understandable.'

'–and I'm running late. So, to what do I owe the pleasure? Is this about the boat?'

'Actually,' said West, 'it's about your daughter, Rhona.'

'Rhona? But I've just told that young lad everything I know.'

'Well, once more won't hurt. Just for me.'

'No disrespect,' said Baxter, 'I mean, I'm happy to have a detective like yourself looking for her, but do you not have more serious crimes to attend to?'

'This is serious,' said West. 'The boys in blue are going to look for her and I am going to try and find out why she disappeared in the first place. That way we might get an idea of where she's gone.'

'Well, in that case,' said Baxter as he opened the door, 'you'd best come in.'

With his wife under strict instructions to remain in the kitchen lest she intoxicate their guests by breathing on them, Baxter headed for the lounge and pointed West in the direction of the sofa.

'I'd offer you a tea,' he said, 'but–'

'I know, you're pushed for time,' said West. 'Don't worry, I'll be as quick as I can. So, when did you realise Rhona was missing?'

'Yesterday,' said Baxter. 'Maureen went to–'

'Maureen?'

'The wife.'

'Is she here?'

'Aye, but she's not up to seeing anyone just now,' said Baxter. 'She can't open her mouth without bursting into tears.'

'Fair enough,' said West. 'Sorry, I interrupted. You were saying.'

'Oh, aye, Maureen. She called Rhona for breakfast and when she didn't answer, that's when she realised she'd gone.'

'And is that unusual? I mean, for Rhona to go out so early?'

'Aye. The girl's happier in her bed than out of it.'

'But you didn't call the police, not straight away?'

'No, no. No point in jumping off the deep end, you know what women are like, probably went to clear her head or something. We waited until lunchtime, or thereabouts, then I went looking for her. Up to the woods, then a drive up the road and back.'

'But no luck?'

'No, I even tried the taxi office but they've not had any fares up here for weeks.'

'Did she a leave a note?' said West. 'Or a message on your phone, maybe?'

'Nothing, Inspector, but what I can't understand is this: if she was of a mind to take a wander, then why did she not take her bag with her? Or her phone?'

'You mean they're still here?'

'Aye, in the den. That's where she's been sleeping.'

'Can we have a look?'

West, still dreaming of the day she'd have her own stone cottage filled with vintage furniture, open fires, and a kitchen with a coal-fired range, was immediately taken by the cosy, antiquated charm of the converted cellar.

'Blimey,' she said, 'this is a right little getaway. I wouldn't mind hiding down here myself.'

'Hiding?'

'Yeah, you know, somewhere where you can cut yourself off from the outside world.'

'Oh aye, peace and quiet, you mean? It's ideal for that.'

'So, if Rhona was sleeping down here, I take it she was just visiting, is that right?'

'Aye. She said she'd stay a few days, no more, but that was three weeks ago.'

'Getting under your feet, was she?'

'Quite the opposite, Inspector. Quite the opposite.'

'Okay, listen,' said West, 'I need to ask a few questions that might sound a bit personal but you don't have to answer them, if you don't want to.'

'What is it you're wanting to know?'

'Well, did Rhona have any problems that you know about? Any financial worries, for example?'

Deeming the envelope evidence enough that money was clearly not one his daughter's problems, Baxter, fearing any mention of its contents would only serve to complicate matters and thereby prolong West's untimely visit, thought it best left unsaid.

'No,' he said bluntly. 'She's on a good wage, by all accounts she earns more than most folk.'

'And no habits? Not fond of the odd drink, perhaps? Drugs?'

'None.'

'And what about personally?' said West. 'I mean, have you noticed anything odd about her behaviour, does she seem alright in herself?'

'A wee bit moody,' said Baxter, 'but otherwise... no, that's not strictly true.'

'Go on.'

'See here, Inspector, Rhona's like her mother, she likes to haver, she could talk the hind legs off a donkey, but from the day she arrived, she's said nothing. She's kept herself to herself.'

'Sounds like something's worrying her. Maybe she's pregnant.'

'It's not that,' said Baxter.

'What is it, then?'

'I wish I knew. We'd not seen her in months, okay? Then she turns up out of the blue, in the middle of the night, if you please. She told Maureen that she'd lost her job and her flat.'

'Oh well, there you go. That's enough to send anyone into the depths of depression. She's probably stressed out about finding somewhere else to live.'

'That's not it!' said Baxter, angrily. 'She's a clever lass, she can get whatever she wants. Now, if she was that bothered about finding somewhere to live, she'd have been shoving that blessed computer under our noses asking our opinion on the flats she was looking at. And another thing, if she'd lost her flat, then why did she not bring her belongings with her? She was empty-handed, Inspector, not even a suitcase. And why was she not looking for work?'

'Well,' said West, trying her best to sound sympathetic, 'maybe she just needed some time out. Maybe she's been thinking about a career change, or moving somewhere else.'

'No, no. I'm telling you, she's up to something, and whatever it is, she's keeping it to herself.'

'What does she do? Work-wise, I mean.'

'The North West Castle,' said Baxter. 'It's a big, fancy hotel in Stranraer, but I've no idea what she does there.'

'Okay. I'll give them a bell later and find out why they let her go. What about partners? I take it she's not married?'

'No. But she has a boyfriend, I think. A fella by the name of Callum.'

'Callum what?'

'Search me. She never said and we never asked.'

'Do they live together?'

'As far as I know, Rhona's always lived alone.'

'I'll need her address,' said West, 'and Callum's, too.'

'Can't help you there,' said Baxter, 'but you could ask him yourself, his number's on the phone.'

Baxter turned his back, opened the ottoman, and produced his daughter's handbag and mobile while West, eyeing the half-eaten bowl of crumble lying on the side, snapped on a pair of gloves.

'Just out of interest,' she said as she unzipped the bag, 'did you mention these to the officer who was here earlier?'

'I did, aye.'

'And he didn't ask to see them?'

'No. Should he have?'

'Most definitely.'

'Will I chase after him?'

'It's too late for that,' said West as she rummaged through the bag. 'Is there anything missing from here? I mean, have you or your wife taken anything out?'

Baxter paused before answering.

'No,' he said, clearing his throat, 'it's as we found it.'

'And the phone?'

'Likewise. You'll see a number there, the last missed call, that was Maureen. She telephoned Rhona when we realised she was missing.'

'And you mentioned a computer,' said West. 'Is that here, too?'

'Aye, her laptop. It's on the shelf behind you.'

'Has anyone used it apart from your daughter?'

'I wouldn't know how,' said Baxter, 'and I'm pretty sure Rhona never touched it the whole time she was here.'

'Good. I'll need to take these with me,' said West. 'Is that alright with you?'

'No bother. Help yourself.'

'Thanks, you can have them back later. Right, I won't keep you any longer. Just so's you know, we'll find out who this Callum geezer is, maybe he can shed some light on her whereabouts, and like I said, I'll have a word with the hotel, too.'

'Much appreciated.'

'I'll be in touch when I have some news. In the meantime, try not to worry, and tell your wife we'll find her, okay?'

* * *

There were, mused West, some folk in life who appeared to enjoy more than their fair share of luck, be it a win on the horses, six numbers on the lottery, or a hefty inheritance following the demise of a wealthy relative but Willy Baxter, having mislaid his daughter within a day or two of discovering the hollow carcass of an Icelandic national, was not one of them.

Feeling a tinge of compassion for the ageing farmer who, if his luck continued, would doubtless contract a debilitating bout of pneumonia by nightfall, she pulled off the main road, Googled the hotel in Stranraer, and dialled.

'Thank you for calling the North West Castle,' came a voice. 'How can I help?'

'Detective Inspector West. I'd like a word with whoever's in charge, please.'

'That's myself. I'm Vince Campbell, the Duty Manager.'

'Hello Vince, it's about one of your staff, a Miss Rhona Baxter.'

'Oh aye, Rhona. She's not here just now, I'm afraid.'

'Well, she wouldn't be,' said West, 'not if you've fired her.'

'I'm sorry?' said Campbell. 'What do you mean, fired?'

'I was told she'd lost her job.'

'Well, if she has, it's not this one.'

'So, she still works there?'

'Of course. And I'll tell you this for nothing, Inspector, if we ever did have to let someone go, she'd be the last.'

'I see. Sorry about that,' said West. 'I must have got my wires crossed. Can you tell me what time she's due in?'

'I wish I could,' said Campbell, 'but we've not seen her in days.'

'Oh?'

'She'd booked some time off but she was due back on Monday, unfortunately, she's still not surfaced.'

'Have you tried calling her?'

'Aye, the landline at home, but no answer. And her mobile a few days ago.'

'And you've no idea where she is?'

'I'm afraid not, but Rhona's not one to shirk. We figured she's probably come down with a wee cold or something, best to leave her in peace, we can cope for now.'

'Quite right,' said West, 'no sense in spreading all those germs around, especially in your line of business.'

'Exactly. If it's not top secret, do you mind me asking if anything's happened? I mean, is Rhona alright?'

'Yeah, nothing to worry about really. It's just her folks, they've been trying to get hold of her too, you know what parents are like.'

'If they're anything like mine, I feel for her.'

'Listen, do you mind if ask you a couple of questions? It won't take long.'

'Aye, go on.'

'Can you tell me exactly what Rhona does at the hotel?'

'Main desk by day,' said Campbell, 'and front of house in the restaurant by evening.'

'And would you say she was good at her job?'

'The best there is. Stylish, impeccable manners, and she's always willing to go that extra mile just to keep the guests happy. In fact, I'd go so far to say she's half the reason most folk come back.'

'So, she's obviously happy at work?'

'Oh, aye, she loves it here.'

'No petty gripes? No problems with management or staff?'

'No, she's well-liked by everyone.'

'I understand she has a boyfriend,' said West, irked by the sudden beep in her ear, 'a bloke called Callum. Do you know him?'

'I didn't even know she had a boyfriend, in fact, that's probably why she's so popular with the lads in the kitchen.'

'Sorry, I'm going to have to leave it there, I've got a call waiting.'

'No bother,' said Campbell, 'happy to help, and be sure to let us know when you find her, I'd hate to think something might have happened.'

'Of course I will,' said West, taking the other call. 'Duncan, how's it going?'

'I thought you might like a wee update on the Boyds, miss. Are you okay to talk?'

'Yeah, how'd it go?'

'Better than good,' said Duncan. 'Henry's not said much, without his brother he seems to lose the gift of speech – he just clammed up.'

'And that's good?'

'It is as far as Jack's concerned. I've charged him with both offences under the Merchant Shipping Act, just like Dougal said.'

'I'm glad to hear it. I don't trust him, he's better off in custody than he is roaming the streets.'

'Oh, there's no chance of that, miss,' said Duncan, 'I've… I've taken a bit of a flyer.'

'I'm not sure I like the sound of this. Go on, let's have it.'

'I've arrested him on suspicion of the murder of Aron Jónsson.'

West, whilst not averse to surprises, particularly those involving a single malt, was not so keen on those which appeared to flaunt the rules of due process.

'You've done what?' she said, raising her voice. 'Have you lost the bleeding plot?'

'Calm your jets, miss!'

'Oh, I really hope you can back this up, Duncan! For God's sake! We haven't got a shred of evidence! We haven't got anything that absolutely, irrefutably, without a shadow of a doubt, incriminates him!'

'We have now.'

West paused for a second and gazed at her phone.

'What do you mean?'

'Well, it's nothing physical, I'll give you that,' said Duncan, 'but I have him on tape. He knew Aron Jónsson was on board the *Thistledonia* when it ran aground, and get this, he also knew he was dead.'

'Oh, for crying out loud! What you mean is, he *assumed* Jónsson was aboard the *Thistledonia*, like he *assumed* Jónsson was the one who nicked the boat in the first place!'

'No, miss! You can hear it for yourself. Jack Boyd *knew for a fact* that Jónsson was dead, and before you ask, no, I didn't push him, and no, I didn't ask any leading questions, he tripped himself up.'

West allowed the craftiest of smiles to creep across her face.

'Well, that's alright then,' she said, 'but listen, we still need to *prove* that he's the perp. We need some hard evidence. I just hope for all our sakes that Dougal and the light of his life find something other than everlasting love at the Boyds' place.'

'Oh, I'm made up for him,' said Duncan, 'it's about time he had something on the end of his line, the poor fella's not had a bite in years. Anyway, they're on their way back so we'll know one way or the other before too long. Oh, and I nearly forgot, McLeod's on his way over, he's got some news.'

'I hope it's better than yours.'

'Where are you, anyway?'

'Baxter's house.'

'Willy Baxter?' said Duncan. 'How so?'

'His daughter went missing yesterday. I thought there might be something in it.'

'But?'

'Nah. Just a coincidence, I think. Don't get me wrong, something's definitely up with the girl but it sounds like boyfriend trouble to me.'

'Well, whatever it is,' said Duncan, 'I feel for old man Baxter, first the boat, then this.'

'Tell me about it. If the poor sod opened a pub, they'd bring back prohibition. Right, I'm going to stick my foot down, I'll be back before you know it. Do me a favour and get some grub in, would you? I'm starving.'

'Roger that,' said Duncan. 'Is there anything in particular you're wanting?'

'Not fussed,' said West. 'But for some strange reason, I do have a yearning for some apple pie and custard.'

Chapter 10

Regarding bachelorhood as a lonely but sure-fire way of safeguarding his daily routine and dogged pursuit of all things piscine, Dougal, though buoyed by the prospect of spending a weekend in the company of Kay Grogan, was characteristically anxious about the inevitable getting-to-know-you conversation where, at the risk of blowing his chances with a female of the species, he'd feel obliged to divulge his passion for ironing, his organisational OCD, and his fear of anything remotely canine.

Saddled with the task of selecting a mutually agreeable activity which would also provide him with an escape route should his nerves get the better of him, he dismissed the notion of an intimate dinner for two, or sitting in a darkened cinema where a straying hand might cause him to jump from his seat, in favour of exploring the secret follies and woodland walks in the grounds of Culzean Castle.

'Well, I think you're mad,' said Duncan as he demolished a BLT. 'Have you not seen the forecast for the weekend? You'd have to be a numpty to go out in that weather.'

'No, no, she likes the outdoors,' said Dougal. 'She's an all-weather girl.'

'And how about you?'

'What do you mean?'

'Face it, pal. One dollop of mud on your trousers and you'll be running home to change.'

'Away!'

'And what about after?'

'I'm not with you.'

'Once you've walked your socks off, and you're both soaked to the skin, what then?'

'I don't know.'

Duncan popped the lid on his takeaway latte, glanced at Dougal, and winked.

'What if she invites you back to her place?'

'Jeez-oh! I'd not thought of that!'

'Worse still,' said Duncan, 'she might be wanting an invitation back to yours. You can't refuse her if she does, she'll think you're odd.'

'But it might be late!'

'Then she'll be wanting to stop the night.'

'I'm getting the fear.'

'Relax,' said Duncan, 'I'm just winding you up. You obviously like each other, you'll be fine.'

'So will I,' said West as she breezed through the door, 'just as soon as I've had something to eat. What have we got?'

'Take your pick,' said Duncan, 'there's a cheese-salad bap or an egg mayonnaise on wholemeal.'

'Are you having a laugh?'

'I am. There's a BLT going begging, or a sausage toastie.'

'Did you get any pie?'

'Aye, and a wee tub of custard.'

'Perfect,' said West. 'Dougal, just so's you know, I've been to see Willy Baxter, his daughter's gone missing so keep an eye out in case anything comes in.'

'Will do, miss.'

'So, have you had a fruitful morning?'

'I have,' said Dougal, 'very fruitful, indeed.'

'Hold up,' said West. 'Where's your mate? Didn't she go with you?'

'She did, aye, but she's away up to Glasgow. She's taken everything we found to forensic services.'

'Blimey, she's keen.'

'Well, as Duncan's arrested the Boyds on suspicion of murder, we'll be needing the results in less than twelve hours. She's pushing to get them analysed straight away.'

'Well, I'm glad someone's on the ball,' said West. 'So, come on then, what did you find?'

Dougal tapped his keyboard and swung the laptop round to face her.

'Here,' he said, 'I've downloaded all the photos I took on my phone so you can see for yourself. Now, do you watch that programme on the telly they call *Cash in the Attic*?'

'Sorry,' said West, 'I don't watch TV, not much, anyway.'

'Well, they could've named it after these fellas. This is a shot of the attic. As you can see, it's full of the usual junk – tea chests, cardboard boxes, and the like – but you'll also notice in the corner there, three nine-packs of toilet tissue.'

'In the attic?' said Duncan. 'Dear, dear, that could be dangerous if you're caught short.'

'Let me give you a detail,' said Dougal, scrolling to the next image. 'You'll see each pack had been opened and resealed with Sellotape and if I zoom in, you'll also see bundles of twenty-pound notes stuffed in the middle of each roll.'

'Got to hand it to them,' said West. 'It's clever.'

'We've not counted them all but there's roughly fourteen hundred quid in each roll, so that's about forty grand in total.'

'Not bad for a day's labouring,' said Duncan. 'What's next?'

'Two pairs of Wellington boots. Both a size ten, both with a chevron tread. Kay, I mean, Miss Grogan, scanned them with the FLS and they're contaminated. Blood.'

'Blinding!' said West. 'I hope it's Aron Jónsson's, that's exactly what we need.'

'Aye, but hold,' said Duncan. 'Sorry, pal, but we seem to be skirting round the issue of the money. Where did that come from?'

'Probably the proceeds of all that laundry they've been washing,' said West. 'Next photo, please.'

'Oh, a black rucksack,' said Duncan. 'Jack Boyd mentioned that during the interview; it belongs to his brother. Some fella tried to steal it and Henry pummelled him to the ground, that's how come he's on a suspended.'

'Well, I'd say whoever tried to nick it, got off lightly,' said Dougal, 'considering what we found inside.'

'Come on,' said West, 'I'm getting excited, what was in it?'

'Picture one, a box of blue disposable gloves. Picture two, a pair of boot socks. And picture three, a knife. Will I tell you why this knife is so special?'

'No need,' said Duncan. 'It's a fisherman's knife. It's used for filleting the guts out of anything that swims. Or not. As the case may be.'

'How did you know that?'

'There was one just like it next to Aron Jónsson's body.'

'Well,' said Dougal, 'the knife is contaminated, too. On to picture three.'

West leaned forward and frowned as she squinted at the screen.

'What the hell is that?' she said. 'It looks like a bleeding radish.'

'I'm not entirely sure myself,' said Dougal. 'It's smooth and rubbery on the outside but hard in the middle, like a wee marble. We've not opened any of them, we'll let FS take care of that.'

'Hold on,' said West. 'Them?'

'Aye, nine in all.'

'Looks like a prune to me,' said Duncan. 'Maybe that's why the toilet roll's in the attic. Did you not get a look at their motor?'

'What motor?'

'They've a big 4x4, was it not in the garage?'

'No, but there was a trailer with a boat on the back.'

'A boat?' said West. 'What kind of boat? You mean, like a canoe or something?'

'Better than that,' said Dougal as he set the next image to fill the screen. 'This is what we call an RIB, miss, a rigid inflatable boat. It's a type of dinghy, not dissimilar to the D class used by the RNLI, just a wee bit smaller, but take a look at the outboard, it's a beauty.'

'I'm sure it is,' said West, 'but you'd better explain before I nod off.'

'This is not the kind of engine you'd have for pootling around a duck pond. It's a Mercury. One hundred and fifty horsepower. On an RIB this size, it'll have you skimming over the water at twenty, twenty-five miles an hour, easy.'

'I know this must be relevant somehow,' said West, 'but please tell me how, exactly.'

'Okay,' said Dougal, 'remember the data we downloaded from the chartplotter and the AIS?'

'Yeah.'

'Then you'll recall I said it looked as though the *Thistledonia* had stopped off-shore before it was scuppered?'

'Okay?'

'Well, let's just say, what if it stopped to meet another boat? A wee boat so's the crew could jump off before she was run aground.'

'Go on.'

'Well,' said Dougal, 'this could be that kind of boat.'

'So, hang on,' said Duncan. 'What you're suggesting is that someone else, a third party, could have powered that dinghy up to Lendalfoot, picked up Jack and Henry Boyd, then taken off again?'

'Aye, maybe,' said Dougal. 'It is still a maybe.'

'That's genius, pal. The question is, where would they have gone with it?'

'Anywhere they like. As long as there's not any rocks to hinder them, they could drag it up a beach, no trouble at all.'

'I drove past a lovely stretch of beach on the way back from Willy Baxter's place,' said West. 'The thing is, would they be able to lift that thing over the Armco by the side of the road?'

'No bother,' said Dougal. 'It's a two-man job but easily done.'

'In that case, that's where we'll have a gander. There might be some tracks on the lead-up to the road.'

* * *

With most callers to the office dispensing with the formality of knocking before entering, West, bemused by the polite rap on the door, turned and smiled as the willowy Andy McLeod stepped gingerly into the office.

'Okay, Charlie?' he said, rubbing his bushy red beard. 'I'm not interrupting, am I?'

'Only lunch,' said West as she polished off the custard.

'Is that what I think it is?'

'Yup.'

'Are you not heating it up?'

'Don't be daft,' said West. 'This is almost as good as cold baked beans.'

'Heathen.'

'Take a pew. Are you hungry?'

'Not if it's custard on offer, no.'

'Relax,' said West, 'this is mine, but there is a spare BLT if you fancy it.'

'Are you not wanting it yourself?'

'Nah, I'm stuffed.'

'That's a first.'

'Steady, mate. Carry on like that and you'll wind up on one of your own slabs.'

'Alright, Doc?' said Duncan, waving a hand. 'How's life in the cold store?'

'I'm dead on my feet. Any chance of a brew?'

'No bother, sit yourself down.'

'So, will I give you the news?'

'Two ticks,' said West as she yanked a laptop from her bag. 'Dougal, this belongs to Baxter's daughter, Rhona. See if there's anything interesting on it, would you?'

'Okey-dokey.'

'And this is her phone. There's a number on there for a geezer called Callum. I need a second name and an address. Right, Andy, give us what you've got.'

As a forensic pathologist working long, unsociable hours, Andy McLeod embraced the opportunity to share in some light-hearted banter with his friends and colleagues during his visits to the office as a welcome respite from the one-sided conversations he'd have with his clients in the mortuary.

Accepting the offer of a sandwich, he removed his coat, pulled a small memo pad from his pocket, and sat down.

'I made myself some notes,' he said, 'you can read the full report as soon as it's available. Okay, let's start with the cause of death. Our friend, Mr Jónsson, suffered two intrusions to the chest, the second entered the intercostal space between T3 and T4 and penetrated the left ventricle where subsequent–'

'Stop!' said West, raising her hands. 'Sorry, Andy, I hate to be a killjoy but can you put it in layman's terms, please.'

McLeod sipped his tea, glanced at West, and smiled.

'He was stabbed,' he said. 'In the heart.'

'Cheers. And the weapon?'

'Well, there's a nice, clean cut on one side of the wound at the point of entry, whilst the other is, shall we say, somewhat ragged. In other words, as we thought, it's a perfect match for the knife we found beside the body.'

'That's smashing,' said Duncan, 'but tell me something, Doc, if he was already dead, then why would they want to butcher him?'

'I've a vague idea,' said McLeod. 'No. In fact, I'm being too modest. I know exactly why they cut him open.'

'Cor blimey,' said West, 'talk about dragging it out! Come on, Andy, speed it up.'

'An analysis of sample fluid taken from the body cavity tested positive for traces of benzoylmethylecgonine.'

West stared at McLeod and raised her eyebrows.

'Cocaine,' he said, as he slid a sealed, plastic bag across the table, 'and for la pièce de résistance, I give you exhibit A.'

'I don't believe it,' said West. 'Another bleeding radish.'

'You mean you've got more?'

'Yeah, Dougal found them. They belong to the blokes who chartered the boat.'

'In that case, Charlie,' said McLeod with a smile, 'I think you've grounds enough to charge them with possession at least, and probably intent to supply, as well. You see, this here is not a radish, it's a balloon, one of two I found in Mr Jónsson's body. The second had already made its way to the large bowel, its journey no doubt expedited by an opening dose of fear. Inside each balloon, double-wrapped in latex, is approximately ten to twelve grams of cocaine.'

'So,' said West, 'you're telling me he swallowed them?'

'Well, he certainly didn't ingest them from the other end. My guess is he'd swallowed more than two, probably a fair few, and that's why they unzipped him.'

'Okay, but that's a bit extreme, isn't it? I mean, for a tiny lump like that, wouldn't it have been easier to let nature take its course?'

'Some things in life,' said Duncan, grinning, 'are definitely not worth waiting for. See here, miss, that nose candy has a street value of roughly forty quid a gram, so that tiny lump, as you put it, is worth four or five hundred quid.'

'Duncan's right,' said McLeod, 'and if he'd swallowed, I don't know, say ten, then it was obviously worth the effort.'

Keen to find a connection between the victim and the alleged perpetrators rather than have to plead with DCI Elliot for an extension to their detention whilst they gather more evidence, West thought for a moment, leaned back in her chair, and ruffled her hair.

'Okay,' she said, 'how about this: McClusky swears blind the *Thistledonia* set sail without a skipper, so, what if the Boyds picked up Jónsson when they stopped in St Kilda. Jónsson's got the drugs, they bring it down here, and they swallow it in case they get caught, but the Boyds get greedy and they want Jónsson's share as well.'

'Oh, I'm not sure about that,' said Duncan. 'I simply can't believe they'd make a trip like that for such a small amount of coke. There is another scenario, however.'

'I'm listening.'

'Maybe Jónsson was simply a courier making sure that the merchandise reached its destination and he was on the rob. Maybe he swallowed those pellets because he wanted some for himself, and maybe the Boyds sliced him open because they wanted it back.'

'That's feasible,' said West. 'Yeah, okay, I could buy that.'

'The thing is,' said Duncan, 'Jack and Henry Boyd are a couple of lightweights, miss, they'd not be involved in a stunt like this on their own, they'd have to be working for somebody else, and I reckon to make a trip like that worth their while, they must have brought back a lot more coke than the wee parcels we found. The question is, where have they hidden it? Who are they working for? And where were they delivering it to?'

'I might have to use my *phone-a-friend*,' said West. 'Jimbo's always got an answer for everything.'

Dougal, a natural multi-tasker with a talent for completing two different tasks on two separate computers whilst simultaneously keeping track of the conversation, spoke without looking up.

'There's only one flaw with that theory,' he said, 'if we're to avoid any loose ends, that is. We need to know where Jónsson got the merchandise from.'

West, pondering just how much Balvenie was left in the bottle at her apartment, stood up, slipped her hands into her pockets, and began to pace the room.

'I should be off,' said McLeod, 'my next patient will be getting warm. I meant to ask, Charlie, how's James? Is he recovering well?'

'Happy as a bunny,' said West, 'especially now he's got the dog.'

'Dog?'

'Yup, a lovely little terrier which means he's getting all the exercise he needs.'

'As long he's not overdoing it,' said McLeod. 'So, are you looking forward to the weekend?'

'Yeah, of course I am!' said West. 'I've got an Icelandic drug mule who's been butchered for offal, a boat that's been beached, and the daughter of a sheep farmer who's gone missing. Should be a belter.'

'I take it you'll not have time for a drink, then?'

'Sorry, Mr McLeod,' said Dougal, 'but I don't think she will.'

'Hold on a minute!' said West. 'Since when did you decide what I–'

'The name you're after, miss, for that Callum fella?'

'Yeah?'

'It's McClusky. Callum McClusky. Same address as Tam.'

West, looking as though she'd received a mild electric shock, glared at Dougal, snatched her coat from the back of the chair and bolted from the room.

'Come on, Duncan!' she said, her voice trailing down the corridor. 'We haven't got all day!'

Chapter 11

As the owner of an imposing, three-storey townhouse with enviable views across the harbour, Tam McClusky was regarded by the folk of Kirkcudbright as a compassionate man of means for whom helping his less able neighbours with a run to the supermarket or even a sub until pension day was never a problem, whilst those in his home town of Dumfries, unaware of his reputation as a kind-hearted philanthropist, continued to give him the widest of berths.

With no chores to attend to, or a boat to inspect, he sat alone in the kitchen devouring a stack of buttered toast whilst studying the form of the runners and riders in the feature race at Musselburgh, oblivious to the hum of the Defender idling outside his door.

Gazing at the house through the rain-speckled windscreen, West, prone to viewing such properties as potential doer-uppers in need of nothing more than a lick of paint and a decent pair of curtains, smiled as her imagination ran riot, while Duncan, surveying the home without the benefit of her rose-tinted spectacles, curled his lip and sneered at the missing roof slates, the weathered paintwork, and the rotting window frames.

'I bet there's beasties in the rafters,' he said, cynically, 'and it's probably riddled with damp as well.'

'What do you mean?' said West. 'It's lovely!'

'It's crumbling, miss! Okay, it's three hundred years old and it has a certain charm, I'll give you that, but trust me, it'll take more than a few quid to sort that place out.'

'Well, if he gets his loo rolls from the same place as the Boyds, he'll have it sorted in no time. Come on. With any luck we'll catch him with his trousers down.'

As someone who'd learned from experience that what often lay behind an unlocked door was a blood-splattered hallway or a ransacked living room, Duncan, glancing cautiously at West, reached beneath his jacket and pulled the expandable baton from his belt as she eased the door open with the back of her hand and called inside.

'Hello, hello! Who's shouting me?' yelled McClusky as he waddled down the hall. 'Oh, it's yourself, Inspector, and you too, Sergeant!'

'Did you know your door was open?' said West.

'My door's always open,' said McClusky, 'folk are always dropping by for one thing or another.'

'I never realised you were such a pillar of the community.'

'Certainly the size of one,' said Duncan, muttering under his breath. 'Can we have a wee word, Mr McClusky? Is that okay?'

'Aye, no bother. I've a pot brewing, that'll take the chill from your bones.'

McClusky led them to the kitchen, poured two mugs of tea, and returned to his seat.

'On your own?' said West.

'Sorry?'

'Where's Mrs McClusky?'

'There is no Mrs McClusky.'

'Sorry,' said West, lowering her eyes. 'I didn't mean to sound rude. When did she… I mean, was it…?'

'Oh, she's not dead!' said McClusky. 'No, no, there's plenty of life in the old boot, yet. We separated. Years ago.'

'That's a relief. A mutual parting of the ways, was it?'

'Let's just say, I had a life-changing experience which afforded her the opportunity to change hers as well.'

'Say no more. I'm not here to pry.'

'Then why are you here?' said McClusky. 'It's not about the *Thistledonia*, that's for sure.'

'Why do you say that?'

'Because you'd not be sitting here if it was. You'd have blurted it out on the doorstep or probably phoned.'

'How very astute,' said West. 'Actually, we're here about a girl, a woman by the name of Rhona Baxter.'

McClusky tore into another slice of toast and smiled as he shrugged his shoulders.

'Sorry, hen,' he said. 'Never heard of her.'

'No, but your son has,' said Duncan. 'Callum.'

'Doesn't surprise me,' said McClusky, 'he's a one for ladies, is Callum, a right chip off the old block in that respect. So, what's the story? Is she pregnant?'

'Not that we know of, but we do need to speak to Callum about her.'

'That's as maybe,' said McClusky, 'but I'm afraid it's not possible, not just now, anyway.'

'How so?'

'He's resting. He's under strict instructions to rest and keep well hydrated.'

'I though he was fine,' said West. 'In fact, I distinctly remember you saying you were going to take him out for a ride on the boat.'

'When he's better,' said McClusky. 'Unfortunately, his recovery's been a wee bit on the slow side.'

'Not that it's any of our business,' said Duncan, 'but what's wrong with him?'

'Flu.'

'Oh, that old chestnut,' said West. 'What you mean is, he caught a cold and went to bed.'

'No, Inspector. What I mean is, he had the flu. Proper flu. He fainted and when I picked him, he was a rag doll in my arms, sweating buckets, too. I ran him to the infirmary and they put him on a drip. Slept for two days, he did.'

'Sorry,' said West, 'sometimes I'm too facetious for my own good.'

'I'll not blame you for that,' said McClusky, 'it's not your fault. Most folk haven't a clue about real flu, they bandy it about as a euphemism for the slightest sniffle.'

'All the same. So, where is he now?'

'Upstairs in his bed.'

'And we really can't see him?'

'No, I'll not wake him for you, or anyone else, Inspector. You understand.'

'Fair enough. Maybe we can try again tomorrow.'

'It must be serious if you're that keen to speak to him.'

'Nah, it'll keep. For now, anyway.'

Duncan, smirking as he noticed West eyeing the last slice of toast, picked up his mug and walked to the window.

'That's some view you have here,' he said. 'Stunning, in fact.'

'Right enough,' said McClusky, 'but it's nothing compared to the summer. You'll not see a sunset like it.'

'I'm sure. Is parking not a wee bit of nightmare here? I mean, it's rammed down there already.'

'Not my problem. I rarely drive these days, but the boy gets the hump if some numpty blocks him in.'

'I'd be the same,' said Duncan. 'What kind of motor has he got?'

'One of those wee fridge vans.'

'Not exactly a bird-puller, is it?' said West with a smile. 'Why's he got one of those?'

'Work,' said McClusky. 'He's a fishmonger, of sorts. Actually, more of a fetcher and a carrier.'

'I don't understand.'

'He collects orders from businesses in the area, buys the fish fresh off the harbour while they're all asleep in their beds, and delivers it to their door.'

'I see,' said West. 'Good business, is it?'

'It stinks, Inspector. Something rotten.'

Duncan craned his neck to the street below and stood transfixed by the antics of a wide-eyed scally in a scarf and tatty jeans who scurried towards the Defender like a crack-head looking for a fix, before turning on his heels and heading back the way he came.

'Your son, Callum,' he said, 'a big fella, is he?'

'Well, he's not got a waist like mine,' said McClusky, 'but height-wise, aye, he's about the same.'

'Must be a looker if he's a hit with the ladies.'

'Aye, he's something of a young Robert Mitchum about him, broad shoulders, big chest, and thick, black hair.'

'And you say he was in the infirmary? Here, in Dumfries?'

'He was, aye.'

'Okay. Well, I think that's us.'

West trying her best to hide the look of confusion on her face, finished her tea and stood.

'Thanks for the brew,' she said. 'We'll drop by tomorrow if that's okay, see if we can't catch up with him then.'

'No bother, Inspector. Drop by anytime you like, anytime at all.'

* * *

Unused to having anyone terminate a meeting other than herself, West fired up the engine, turned to Duncan, and frowned inquisitively.

'Come on, then,' she said. 'Why the sudden exit?'

'If I told you, miss, you'd think I was mad.'

'Try me.'

'Okay, Tam McClusky just gave us a description of his son, did he not?'

'So?'

'He was here. Just now.'

'Where?'

'Right here,' said Duncan. 'He was casing the car like some kind of chancer then took off up the way.'

'You're sure?'

'Positive. Look, I know it sounds daft, miss, but I'm not convinced Callum McClusky's lying in his bed. And I'm not convinced he's got the flu, either.'

'So, what do you want to do?'

'I think we should go to the infirmary,' said Duncan, 'and ask a few questions.'

* * *

Embracing the art of delegation, West waited patiently in the Defender with a half-empty bag of Moffat toffee until Duncan, racing across the sodden car park, returned with a grin on his face.

'So, how'd you get on?' she asked.

'Well, McClusky wasn't lying about bringing his boy to the A&E. He was here alright.'

'Well, there you go,' said West, 'talk about over-reacting.'

'But he didn't have the flu, miss. And they didn't keep him in, either. They stitched him up and sent him on his way.'

'Stitched him up?'

'Callum McClusky was treated for a stab wound to the neck and two to the upper arm.'

'You what?'

'Which would explain why he was wearing a scarf.'

'Yeah but hold on,' said West, 'if that's the case, then why's his old man covering for him with some cock and bull story about the flu?'

'Maybe Callum's a chip off the old block in more ways than one.'

'Okay,' said West, unwrapping another toffee, 'let's think about this for a moment. Rhona Baxter and Callum McClusky definitely had something going on, right?'

'Right.'

'She goes missing, and he's been stabbed, so what do you think? Some kind of mutual retribution? Or was a third party involved?'

'There's only one way to find out,' said Duncan, 'we're going to have to speak to him.'

'Exactly. Right, get uniform to pick him up and tell Dougal to sort out a warrant too, just in case we need to–'

'Steady, miss! I think you're forgetting something.'

'What?'

'We're in Dumfries and Galloway,' said Duncan, 'not Ayrshire! We'll have to put in a request for D&G to pick him up.'

'Oh, for God's sake!' said West as she thumped the wheel. 'We don't have time for that!'

'We've not much choice.'

'Then you'd better give them a bell,' said West, 'and while you do that, I'm going to use my *phone-a-friend*.'

Chapter 12

Aware that DS Dougal McCrae, the walking epitome of diligence personified, had little in his life apart from the lure of brown trout to keep him from his desk, both West and Duncan were nonetheless surprised to find him alone in the office poring over a print-out with a gleeful expression on his face.

'Blimey, you still here?' said West. 'I thought you'd be ordering your chicken chop suey by now.'

'No, no. I'm waiting on Kay, miss. She said she'd call as soon as the first results came in.'

'You make it sound like Eurovision,' said West. 'What are you looking so happy about, anyway?'

Dougal leaned back in his seat and grinned as he waved a sheet of A4 in the air.

'I've had an update from the Icelandic embassy,' he said. 'This is from the police in Hvolsvöllur.'

'If you say so.'

'Aron Jónsson's been under surveillance for almost a year.'

'How so?' said Duncan. 'Has he got form?'

'No, and that's precisely why they've been watching him. He's well known to the authorities but they've nothing on him, he's not got a single conviction.'

'Get to the point, pal. What are they after him for?'

'Cocaine,' said Dougal, 'the supply, thereof. They know he's dealing but he's clever, he leaves enough false trails to drive a bloodhound to distraction. Apparently, they've raided his home four times this year and found nothing, and get this, they even tried to collar him at work.'

'I'm surprised he didn't do them for harassment,' said West. 'So, what did he do, then? Work-wise, I mean.'

'You'll like this,' said Dougal, 'he was a trawlerman. Guess where.'

'Well, Iceland, obviously.'

'On board the *Loki*, miss.'

West slumped in her seat, swung her feet onto the desk, and stared at Dougal as she waited for the penny to drop.

'Give me a minute,' she said, 'I know the name but I can't place it.'

'The stern trawler!' said Dougal. 'Remember? St Kilda?'

'Well, blow me down! So, you were right all along!'

'No, no,' said Dougal. 'I made an assumption based on the evidence to hand and concluded that there was simply a likelihood that the *Thistledonia* went to meet the *Loki*. I never said for sure.'

'You know what they say about the meek inheriting the earth?'

'Aye?'

'You're one of them.'

'So,' said Duncan, 'if we put all this together, then what we're saying is that the Boyds headed up to St Kilda for no other reason than to meet Jónsson?'

'It certainly seems that way, aye.'

'Okay,' said West, 'slow down, it's late, I'm tired, and without a Balvenie to prop me up, the old grey matter's fading fast. So, Jónsson's on the *Loki* and his role as a trawlerman is just a front, right?'

'Correct.'

'And just to be straight, Jónsson was carrying a shipment of coke and the Boyds went to meet him, and they all came back together?'

'Well, if there's another reasonable explanation,' said Dougal, 'I'm afraid it's not one I'm familiar with.'

West buried her face in her hands and sighed before checking her watch.

'Alright,' she said, wearily, 'let's pick this apart. If Jack and Henry Boyd were there to collect the merchandise, then why did Jónsson sail back with them? I mean, why not just hand it over?'

'Well, if it was a sizeable amount,' said Duncan, 'then there's always the possibility that he wanted to be sure it reached its final destination.'

'Which brings me to my next question,' said West. 'Who was he flogging it to? I mean, what was the final destination?'

'Don't ask me,' said Duncan, 'my head's mince, but I will say this, Jack Boyd's the monkey here, there's an organ grinder behind this operation and that's the fella we need to find.'

'And Jack Boyd,' said West, 'is the only one who knows who that is. We need to have another word.'

'Good luck with that, miss. He's not saying anything just now. Maybe we should wait for a result on his gear from FS.'

'Okay,' said West. 'Agreed. If we get something positive, then maybe a charge of murder will loosen his tongue. Right, I say it's time we shoved off. Duncan, get going, you've earned yourself a pint.'

'Roger that, miss.'

'Dougal?'

'I'm stopping here. I don't want to miss Kay when she calls.'

'Well, give me a bell as soon as you hear anything, good or bad, and I will see you in the…'

Whilst the occasional clamour of footsteps clumping along the corridor was to be expected, and the murmur of muffled voices a regular occurrence, the baritone bark of something resembling the Hound of the Baskervilles was unusual enough to make Dougal raise his feet from the floor and recoil in terror as the door inched its way open to reveal a small, Scottish terrier pursued by a chipper-looking Munro.

'Good to see you, chief!' said Duncan. 'You're looking well!'

'Likewise, laddie,' said Munro as he shook his hand. 'I see you're burning the midnight oil again, Charlie.'

'What the hell are you doing here?'

'Well, with all the rustling of the leaves on the trees I was convinced there was a storm brewing but as there are no leaves in my neck of the woods I realised the racket was probably down to a collective scratching of heads.'

'Nothing wrong with your hearing, then.'

'Nor your inimitable knack of making a visitor feel at home.'

'Sorry, Jimbo,' said West, smiling apologetically, 'it's been one of those days, *been* being the operative word. We're shoving off.'

'I see my sense of timing is as impeccable as ever.'

'Hold up, you're not driving all the way back to Carsethorn, now, are you?'

'I should hope not, I've only just arrived.'

'Good,' said West, as she zipped her coat, 'then you and Murdo can crash at mine. I've been trying to get hold of you anyway.'

'How so?'

'I'll explain on the way, but first we need to collect your mate Angus from Aberdeen and a decent bottle of red.'

* * *

Mindful of the fact that any negative comments on the subject of West's slatternly housekeeping skills would result in a defensive diatribe on the perils of being a time-strapped professional living alone, Munro, ignoring the piles of clothes strewn along the hallway and the crusty dishes cluttering the sink, opened the patio doors in a bid to clear the smoke emanating from the frying pan, uncorked the wine, and took a seat at the table while Murdo, more interested in the burnt offering on his master's plate than his own chewy treat, sat salivating by his side.

'So, seriously,' said West, crunching through a forkful of French fries, 'why did you come all the way up here? You can't be bored, not with Murdo.'

'I'm nothing of the sort, Charlie. I had a wee errand to run, that's all.'

'Top secret, is it?'

'If you must know, I had to visit the pet superstore on Alloway Street where I procured a winter coat for my wee companion in a rather fetching Royal Stewart tartan.'

'Oh, come off it!' said West. 'You're not fooling me, Jimbo. Are you trying to tell me there isn't a pet shop in Dumfries?'

'Och, I dare there is, lassie, but where, I'll never know.'

'Just look it up on the internet!'

'You forget,' said Munro, 'I do not possess a computer, nor do I have any desire to own such a device and in the absence of what we used to call *the telephone book*, it's simply easier to go somewhere I'm familiar with.'

'Alright, I'll let you off,' said West, 'but are you sure that's the only reason?'

'Correct me if I'm wrong,' said Munro, 'but was it not *you* that was trying to get a hold of me?'

'Guilty as charged.'

'So, what's the story?'

'Same old,' said West. 'I just needed to bounce things round a bit.'

'Well, that's why you have Dougal and Duncan.'

'I know, I know. Don't get me wrong, I'm not knocking them, they're diamonds, but it's experience they're lacking.'

'Not unlike yourself, lassie.'

'Exactly. And I'm not ashamed to admit it.'

'And you dinnae mind discussing the case with a codger like myself?'

'You're nothing of the sort,' said West, 'and might I remind you, you're still employed, if that's the right word, as a volunteer so if I need some objective, rational advice, who better to ask?'

'Not a politician,' said Munro, 'but I could think of a few folk who'd be willing to listen.'

'Yeah, but which one of them would have *anything and everything* as their specialist subject on Mastermind?'

'Carry on like that,' said Munro, draining his glass, 'and I shall have to buy a bigger hat. Right, let's have it, Charlie; to the point, mind, no havering.'

'Okay, in a nutshell, the dead bloke on the boat?'

'Aye?'

'He's from Iceland. He's a drug dealer. And we think he was on the boat to make sure his merchandise was delivered safely.'

Munro topped up the wine, took a large sip, and gazed pensively at the cobwebs hanging from the light fitting.

'Perhaps,' he said, 'but there could be another reason.'

'I'm all ears,' said West. 'Come on, let's have it.'

'I cannae recall a transaction of this sort ever being settled with a cheque or a bank transfer, so perhaps he was guarding his property until he was paid in full.'

'Now that,' said West, raising her glass, 'is exactly what I'm talking about. Cheers, Jimbo. Now, see if you can answer this one.'

'On you go.'

'When McLeod had him on the slab, he found a couple of pellets in his guts, or what was left of them – balloons actually. Each one was stuffed with about half a grand's worth of coke.'

'And?'

'Well,' said West, 'we reckon the two blokes who chartered the boat, Jack and Henry Boyd, knew he'd swallowed it and wanted it back, presumably so they didn't get it in the neck from whoever they were meant to be delivering it to.'

'Sounds logical,' said Munro, 'so what's your problem?'

'Flipping heck, Jimbo! I thought you'd be ahead of me by now! The problem is, why the hell would this geezer swallow his own merchandise?'

Munro slipped Murdo the tiniest slither of burnt steak and smiled as it disappeared, hardly touching the sides.

'Sometimes, Charlie,' he said, pushing his plate to one side, 'it's better to take things at face value rather than over-analyse them.'

'What do you mean?'

'It sounds to me as if this fellow on the boat was guilty of nothing more than executing a familiar ploy popular amongst the good, the bad, and the greedy, otherwise known as fleecing the customer, short-changing them, ripping them off. Two thousand pounds' worth of cocaine in his belly is an extra two thousand pounds in the bank, once he's sold it on to somebody else.'

'Yeah but why?' said West. 'I mean, he's probably got tons of the stuff.'

'Aye, he probably has. All weighed out and packaged into wee parcels. Not that easy to pull out of your pocket if some junkie on the harbour wants a wee shot.'

'You think so?'

'It's a theory, Charlie. And based on my knowledge of how these folk operate, I'd say it was a reliable one at that.'

West went to the fridge, removed two individual sticky toffee puddings and popped them into the microwave before returning to the table.

'Alright,' she said, 'but assuming what he swallowed was just a tiny fraction of the entire shipment, is it really worth killing someone to get it back?'

'You're talking about the Boyds, of course?'

'Yup.'

'Then put yourself in their shoes,' said Munro. 'If they were acting as couriers, how do you think their boss would react if he discovered part of his shipment was missing?'

'Well, if they'd been doing this on a regular basis, then I reckon he'd probably have a hissy fit, give them a slap on the wrist, and send them home.'

'Wrong. If they'd been doing this on a regular basis, then the chances are that their boss would conclude that they'd been ripping him off on a regular basis, too. Trust me, lassie, those two boys were probably fearing for the use of their legs, so in order to avoid a future on wheels, they retrieved it the only way they knew how.'

West pursed her lips as she pondered the scenario.

'You're not convinced, are you?' said Munro.

'Yes and no,' said West. 'I get what you're saying, Jimbo, but what I cannot get my head around is why they had to butcher the poor bloke? I mean, why not just bosh him over the head and wait for nature to take its course?'

'Circumstances,' said Munro. 'You're in the middle of the ocean, in the dead of the night, with a known drug dealer on your boat, and another waiting for you on the mainland. That is what I'd call being caught between a rock and a hard place.'

'Maybe,' said West, as the microwave pinged. 'Maybe.'

'And the Boyds, are you any nearer to securing a conviction?'

'We're waiting on forensics,' said West. 'If they don't come up trumps, we've had it. They'll end up walking away with a fine or maybe a custodial for scuppering the boat, but that's about it. And as for the drugs, we haven't the foggiest where they were going or who the buyer is.'

'I can feel your pain, lassie, not least because that's not the extent of your worries, is it?'

'What do you mean?'

'Come, come, Charlie. You'd not be calling me for something like this. What's the real point of this conversation?'

West took a deep breath and cleared her throat.

'The bloke who discovered the boat,' she said, 'Willy Baxter. His daughter's gone missing. According to Dumfries and Galloway–'

'Dumfries?'

'She lives in Stranraer,' said West, 'not far from the hotel where she works. Anyway, they had a mooch around her flat and apart from the mail on the doormat, everything's normal. The wardrobe's full of clothes, and there's even a coffee mug left on the kitchen counter.'

'So?'

'So according to Baxter and his missus, she said she'd lost the flat; she said she'd had to give it up but she was clearly intent on going back.'

'Either that,' said Munro, 'or she left in a hurry.'

'The thing is, she was tight with some geezer called Callum but we don't know how close they were. Her parents claim he was the boyfriend but her workmates say she was single.'

'Keep going.'

'This Callum bloke,' said West, 'his second name's McClusky.'

Munro raised his head, narrowed his steely blue eyes, and glared across the table.

'The same–?'

'Yes! The same! Tam McClusky's his father.'

'You're treading dangerous waters, lassie. Watch your back.'

'I know, I know. That's why I was calling you.'

'And McClusky junior, have you invited him in for a wee chat?'

'We would if we could find him,' said West. 'The problem is, he's in Kirkcudbright. We had to get back to D&G and ask them to pick him up but they haven't got back to us yet. To be honest, I've got a horrible feeling he's done a bunk.'

'What makes you think that?'

'Tam McClusky said Callum was ill in bed. He'd been in the infirmary overnight with a bad case of the flu.'

'I'm not surprised,' said Munro. 'Folk dinnae realise just how debilitating flu can be.'

'It wasn't the flu,' said West. 'Duncan checked. He was in the infirmary alright, but he was in A&E. They treated him for multiple stab wounds.'

'And what do you make of this, Charlie? About the Baxter girl going missing and this friendship with McClusky?'

West glanced at Munro, took a sip of wine and shook her head.

'Oh, here we go,' she said, laughing. 'Are you implying that this is all somehow connected? Come on, Jimbo, it's a coincidence, that's all.'

Munro left the table, closed the patio doors, and stood staring at his reflection with his hands clasped behind his back.

'Far be it for me to interfere with your investigation,' he said, 'but should you not be looking at the bigger picture?'

'I'm not with you.'

'Good grief, Charlie! You're not that stupid! Think, lassie, think! See here, McClusky owns the boat that ran ashore, okay? The boat was carrying a shipment of drugs. And then the daughter of the fellow who discovered the boat goes missing. Not only is she involved with Callum McClusky, but then he's treated for stab wounds in the hospital and you think this is all coincidence? No offence, Charlie, but you're better than that! I suggest you get some rest, maybe then you'll start thinking like the consummate professional I know you are!'

'That's me told.'

Munro took his plastic pot of steaming hot dessert from the table and moved to the sofa where he was swiftly joined by his loyal, though some might say, excessively needy, companion.

'Lecture over,' he said. 'You need to take your mind off matters so I suggest we change the subject.'

'Easier said than done. You know what it's like.'

'Nonsense,' said Munro. 'So, have you had yourself a date with Dr McLeod, yet?'

'You what?' said West, choking on her dessert.

'Well, he's been champing at your heels for months, has he not?'

'Are you for real?' said West. 'Can't we play Monopoly, instead?'

'What are you so scared of, Charlie?'

Shocked by the honesty of his question, West, reeling as though the nerve he'd touched was the one normally found in the root canal, stared blankly back across the table.

'Dunno,' she said, softly. 'Once bitten, and all that.'

'Well, see here,' said Munro, 'you listen to me. Andy McLeod's not like your ex, lassie. He's not a thief, or a druggie, and he's not a philanderer. He's a decent chap.'

'Yeah, alright,' said West. 'Blimey, it's like being on the flipping couch. Look, Jimbo, I get what you're saying, and I appreciate your concern, but the bottom line is, I just don't know if I fancy him.'

'Well, excuse me for being blunt, Charlie, but let's face it, you're not getting any younger.'

'God, you're a real bag of laughs, you are!'

'All I'm saying is, looks aren't everything.'

'That's what I tell myself every time I look in the mirror.'

'Wheesht! You're a fine-looking woman!' said Munro. 'There's plenty of fellows who'd snap you up if you'd give them a chance, Dr McLeod being one, and God knows, the man could do with warming up.'

'You say all the right things.'

'I do,' said Munro, 'just not at the right time. Okay, lecture over, it's time wee Murdo was in his bed, and I'm inclined to do the same.'

* * *

Left to ruminate on the sofa, West conceded that, though no Steve McQueen, the lofty Andy McLeod, with his wrinkled, pallid complexion, unruly, russet hair, and a chin like a ski slope, did possess a certain rugged, Celtic charm and, as someone used to wielding a scalpel with the utmost precision, was probably good with his hands but any thought of succumbing to his offer of a drink was rudely interrupted by the appearance of an unknown number on her phone.

'West,' she said, wary of disturbing Munro.

'Inspector. It's PC Villiers. I thought you should know we've found the Baxter girl.'

'Oh, thank God for that. Nice one, constable. Where was she? In the boozer with her mates?'

'No, miss. She was in the burn. And she was on her own.'

West scribbled a note for Munro, left it on the dining table, and slipped silently from the flat.

Chapter 13

As a direct result of her parents' relentless pursuit of a vegetarian lifestyle, West – having survived her formative years on a diet of Puy lentils and carrot cake – soon developed the sensory perception of a broody barn owl, a talent which in later years enabled her to pluck a brace of steak bakes from the bottom of a bag of groceries in total darkness. However, trying to locate Balcreuchan Burn on an unlit A77 with nothing but shadowy grassland to the left and the murky waters of the Firth of Clyde to the right, was proving something of a nightmare.

Slowing to a crawl, she pulled her phone from her hip, switched it to speaker, and stabbed recall.

'Inspector,' said PC Villiers. 'Are you on the way?'

'I'm approaching Lendalfoot,' said West. 'Just how far up this bleeding road are you?'

'Aim for Ballantrae, miss. You're looking for Balcreuchan Burn, the road runs over it.'

'Okay, cheers. Shouldn't be too hard to spot a river, I suppose.'

'Oh, it's not a river,' said Villiers, 'it's a tiny, wee stream.'

'What? Well, how the hell am I supposed to find that? It's pitch black out here!'

'Just look for the floodlights and the roadblock, Inspector. You'll not miss it.'

* * *

Without a SOCO to document the scene and a pressing urgency to recover the cadaver as soon as possible, Dr Andy McLeod, working by the glare of an arc light, set about photographing the victim who, despite the weather, was wearing nothing more than a pair of jeans, scuffed trainers, and a crew neck sweater.

Squatting beside the body, he returned the camera to his pocket and gave the voice recorder a running commentary of his observations.

'IC1, female,' he said, 'approximately thirty to thirty-five years of age, lying prostrate in an easterly direction towards the flow of the burn with the left side of her head just above the water level. The victim's sustained a trauma between the temple and the left ear. Injury consists of superficial grazing and a wee cut roughly two centimetres in length. There is evidence of some blood loss but nothing major. There are subcutaneous contusions present on the back of the neck which I am now examining…'

McLeod cradled the head in both hands and gently rotated it, first from side to side, then back and forth, before carefully laying her down again.

'Okay,' he said, matter-of-factly, 'suspected fracture to the C2 which, despite the victim's proximity to the road, is not commensurate with a fall. Note to self: MRI as soon as. The deceased is also exhibiting some discolouration to the cheeks, lips, and extremities indicative of a lack of oxygen, probably the result of asphyxiation caused by the abnormal presence of fluid in the lungs–'

'Is this a private party?' said West. 'Or can anyone join in?'

'Charlie, it's yourself! We can't go on meeting like this.'

'You should've brought a hip flask, we could've made a night of it.'

'Is that an invitation?'

'Maybe,' said West. 'So, how long have you been here?'

'Long enough. Forty, forty-five minutes, or thereabouts.'

'How come you always get here before me?'

'Because,' said McLeod, 'nine times out of ten, Charlie, I'm not having my supper or enjoying a glass of wine when the call comes in. In fact, most nights the only red I get to see is O-positive.'

'Very funny. Okay, first question, how do we know for sure that this is Rhona Baxter?'

McLeod stood and clambered to the road.

'She was carrying a photo ID in her back pocket,' he said, removing his mask. 'Constable Villiers has it, he's waiting for you in the car.'

'Well, he can wait a bit longer,' said West. 'What's the ID for?'

'A hotel. The North West something or other.'

'That's good enough for me,' said West, 'that's where she worked. Anything else?'

'Some loose change and a set of house keys.'

West paused for a moment, folded her arms and stood staring at Baxter's lifeless body.

'Not exactly dressed for a yomp in the woods, is she?'

'She most certainly is not,' said McLeod. 'And I don't believe for a moment that she was. Yomping, that is.'

'So, what do you reckon?'

'Well, first of all, she's a nasty, wee gash to the side of her head. I'd say she got that when she tumbled from the road to the burn.'

'So, you think she fell?'

'Not at all,' said McLeod. 'I think she was pushed.'

'Go on.'

McLeod took West by the arm and guided her towards the burn.

'See here, Charlie,' he said, pointing at the body, 'for a start, she's too far from the road. If she'd tripped and fallen, she'd be right here below us, not a few feet away.'

'And?'

'And it feels as though she has a hangman's fracture.'

'I like the sound of that,' said West, grinning. 'What is it?'

'It's a break in the second vertebra just below the skull, so called for obvious reasons.'

'So, a broken neck, then?'

'Aye.'

'I didn't think they were altogether fatal.'

'They're not,' said McLeod. 'It's a common enough injury, especially amongst sportsmen and victims of whiplash.'

'But?'

'But assuming she wasn't involved in an RTC, or playing rugby at the time of the accident, I'd say somebody broke it for her–'

'Ouch.'

'–either the result of a choke hold, or a hand placed directly beneath the chin, then forcibly snapping it back.'

West, shielding her eyes from the blinding light of the lamp, glanced up and down the deserted road before confronting McLeod with an inquisitive frown.

'Okay,' she said, 'if your theory's right, if she was with someone, someone who broke her neck, then what the hell were they doing wandering round here in the dead of night?'

'No-one in their right mind would be out here on foot, Charlie, and certainly not at night. This is pure hypothesis, of course, but I'm inclined to believe that was she was probably dragged from a car then pushed into the burn.'

'So, she was dead when she hit the water?'

'Dear God, I doubt it,' said McLeod, shaking his head. 'No, no, chances are she was still very much alive.'

'You're sure?'

'Aye, two reasons, Charlie. First of all, the bruising to her neck. For a contusion to appear the body would have to be functioning near enough as normal, it's a part of the healing process. If she was dead, there'd be no bruises.'

'And the second reason?'

'Naturally, I'll have to wait for the results of a scan,' said McLeod, 'but I'm guessing if it's not just the C2 with a fracture but the C3 as well, then that could have damaged the spinal cord which would have rendered her immobile from the waist up, and possibly speechless, too. If she didn't pass out when she bashed her head on the rock, then it was just a matter of time before she succumbed to the cold. Unfortunately for her, when she hit the water, she ended up facing the wrong way. She's probably got half the burn in her lungs.'

'Poor cow,' said West, 'so, not only was she in pain, but she drowned to death?'

'Right enough. Not a pleasant way to go, being paralysed and unable to do anything about it.'

'And how long do you reckon she's been here?'

McLeod glanced at West and scratched the back of his head.

'That's not an easy one, Charlie,' he said. 'Going by the colour of the bruises on her neck, the bluish tinge to her lips, and then factoring in the weather conditions, I could hazard a guess at anywhere between eighteen and thirty-six hours.'

'Well, that sort of coincides with when she went missing,' said West. 'So, the question is, if she didn't get here on foot, then who the hell brought her here?'

'Sorry,' said McLeod, 'I can give you the how and when, Charlie, but the whys and wherefores are your department.'

West took a step forward, slipped her hands into her pockets, and stared blankly at the back of Baxter's sodden head.

'Just thinking out loud,' she said, softly. 'You say she had her ID on her, but no cash and no cards, just some loose change?'

'Aye, that's it.'

'So, chances are it wasn't a taxi because she wouldn't have been able to pay for it, so it must have been someone she knew.'

'Makes sense to me.'

'And if she was carrying her pass, and they were travelling in this direction, then maybe she was on her way back to Stranraer. Either back home, or to the hotel.'

'There you go,' said McLeod, 'you're halfway there already. Now, I don't want to sound rude, Charlie, but I need to fish this young lady out of the water and get her into the wagon.'

'No worries,' said West. 'Thanks Andy, let me know if you find anything and do me a favour, get her profile on the system as soon as you can. I'll leave you in peace, I need to give the hotel a tinkle.'

* * *

Ignoring a surly-looking Villiers and his arm-waving request to join him in the car, West hid behind the Defender and dialled.

'North West Castle, Moira Lewis speaking, how can I help?'

'Hello,' said West, 'I don't suppose one of your managers is about, is he? Vince Campbell?'

'No, no. Not at this time of night. He'll be here at ten, if you'd like to call back then.'

'No, it's alright, you'll do. I'm Detective Inspector West, I was chatting with him earlier. It's about Rhona Baxter.'

'Oh aye, Rhona. What is it you're wanting?'

'You must know about work rosters and the like, was Rhona due back at some point today? Or yesterday, perhaps?'

'Sorry,' said Lewis, 'as far as I know, she's on her holidays.'

'So she's still not called in?'

'Not that I'm aware of.'

'Okay, listen,' said West, 'you might have more of an insight into this than your Mr Campbell. Is Rhona friendly with anyone in particular at the hotel?'

'No, she has a wee gas with everyone.'

'So, no best mates? No-one she might hang around with after work?'

'Not really,' said Lewis. 'Oh, just a minute, there's Alex, maybe. Aye, she definitely gets on well with Alex.'

'Alex who?'

'Alex Dunbar. He's a young lad, mid-twenties.'

'And what does he do?'

'Kitchen porter.'

'And they're good mates, are they?'

'Aye, that's one way of putting it.'

'Sorry?'

'Between you and me,' said Lewis, 'I think they're at it.'

'Really? What makes you say that?'

'I've seen the way they look at each other and…'

'And what?' said West.

'I don't know if I should say.'

'Oh, I think you should.'

'I've seen them together, once or twice, in the town.'

'And does he drive?'

'Oh aye,' said Lewis. 'Nothing fancy, but it goes.'

'And when's he due in?'

'He's on nights just now, so let me see, he'll be starting at four and finishing at one.'

'Nice one,' said West. 'I'll be in touch.'

* * *

Accepting enforced overtime, sleep deprivation, or a lack of sustenance as credible reasons for any display of apathy, West, rolling her eyes as Villiers lethargically waved a sealed, plastic bag from the window of his patrol car, was less forgiving when it came to a blatant disregard for rank or gender.

'Don't get up,' she said as she snatched the pouch from his hand, 'you might do yourself an injury. Is this everything?'

'Aye, miss,' said Villiers with a yawn. 'That's your lot.'

'Have you searched the surrounding area?'

'We're not badgers, miss. We'll have to wait until morning.'

'Well, come first light,' said West, impatiently, 'I want a sweep of this road, at least a mile in each direction.'

'A mile?'

'And I want a SOCO to carry out a detailed search of the area by the burn, got that?'

'Aye,' said Villiers, 'loud and clear, but is that not your responsibility? I mean, no offence, miss, but I'm just–'

West bent forward and leaned into Villiers, causing him to retreat from the window.

'Listen, sunshine,' she said with snarl, 'I've got two dead bodies, a drug smuggler, and a bereft family to deal with, so make the call and get it sorted before I lose my rag, got it?'

Pondering the penalty for insubordination, and deeming death by firing squad perhaps a little too severe, West, sitting in the draughty Defender, helped herself to the last of the toffees, checked her watch, and groaned as the phone rang again.

'Dougal!' she snapped. 'What do you want?'

'Sorry, miss. I've been calling but you're not picking up. Did I wake you?'

'What? No! I'm with McLeod!'

'Sorry, I never realised you were on a date.'

'I'm not on a date!' said West, clenching her teeth. 'We've found the Baxter girl!'

'Jeez-oh!' said Dougal. 'At this time of night? That doesn't sound good.'

'It isn't. She's brown bread.'

'Oh, dear. So, what's the plan?'

'I'm heading up to Baxter's gaff in a bit to break the good news.'

'Rather you than me.'

'Thanks for that. Okay, listen, here's what I need. The North West Castle Hotel–'

'Aye?'

'–there's a geezer there called Alex Dunbar, he's a kitchen porter. I need D&G to either have a word with him or send him over to us.'

'Right you are.'

'He won't be there until four this afternoon. Tell them we need to know his whereabouts over the last forty-eight hours.'

'Is he in the frame, then?'

'Could be.'

'And if he's not talking?'

'Then have a word with The Bear, I know it's pushing the boundaries but tell him we have reasonable grounds to arrest him on suspicion of abduction and murder, and ask him to sort it.'

'No bother,' said Dougal, 'I'll take care of it now.'

'Oh, and tell them they'll need a SOCO, too. He's got a motor. We're looking for beige-coloured fibres off a woollen sweater and any footprints in the footwell, and while they're at it, Rhona Baxter's flat, they need to go over it with a fine-tooth comb.'

'Is that it?'

'One more thing,' said West, 'while you're on the blower, ask them where they are with Callum McClusky, they should have found that bugger by now. Right, that's me done, how are you? You must be knackered.'

'No, no,' said Dougal. 'I'm fine, miss. Really.'

'Well, you don't sound very happy. I take it that means you've not heard from Kay, yet?'

'On the contrary, miss. That's why I was calling. We've a result.'

'Oh, for God's sake!' said West. 'Why didn't you say so instead of letting me waffle on! Come on, then! What is it?'

'The DNA sample taken from Boyd's boot, it's a perfect match for Aron Jónsson.'

'Yes! Get in there! What the hell took them so long?'

'That's Kay's fault, miss.'

'Don't tell me she stopped for a fish supper on the way?'

'No, no,' said Dougal. 'She wanted to be absolutely sure the boot belonged to Boyd so they analysed the whole thing, sliced it open, and retrieved several fibres stuck to the insole. The fibres match the pair of socks we found in the rucksack.'

'Are you serious?'

'Well, that's Kay for you, miss. Fastidious to a fault.'

'Tell you what, mate, if I were you, I'd cancel any plans you have for the weekend and get yourself off to the jewellers.'

'How so?'

'To buy the girl a ring, you dummy! I'm telling you, you and her, it's a match made in heaven.'

'Oh, I'm not so sure, I mean, we haven't even–'

'I'm winding you up!' said West. 'Now, what about the other stuff? The knife, and those balloon-type things?'

'Still waiting, miss. Shouldn't be long now.'

'Well, it looks as though we've made it by the skin of our teeth,' said West. 'Okay, look, I know it's late, I know you've not slept, and I know you're probably starving, but I need you to make yourself useful while you wait for Kay.'

'No bother,' said Dougal. 'Fire away.'

'Get cracking on the report for the fiscal, I want it on her desk first thing, but before you do that, get hold of Duncan. If he's not hammered, tell him to get his backside into the office and charge the Boyds, then he's to meet me at the Baxter's gaff.'

'Any particular reason, miss?'

'Yeah, I could do with some support,' said West. 'I'm not exactly tactful when it comes to breaking bad news.'

'See here,' said Dougal, 'Duncan's not twenty minutes up the road from you, why don't I send him straight there? You can leave the rest to me.'

'Top man,' said West, 'oh, and Dougal, one last thing. Tell him to bring food. I'm starving.'

Chapter 14

Following the discovery of a body below the ruins of Greenan Castle, the rookie DC Duncan Reid – whose leisure time had hitherto consisted of watching football in the pub followed by a late night vindaloo and twelve hours' recovery on the sofa – had realised there was more to life when smitten by the single mother who'd happened across the decaying corpse whilst searching for sea shells with her son.

Forsaking the hangovers in favour of relaxing with his newly acquired, oven-ready family, he'd grown accustomed to home-cooked meals, early nights and, work permitting, weekends spent foraging in the woodlands with Cathy and her budding entomologist of a son.

By the same token, both Cathy and her son were used to the fact that as a DS the term 'shift' was not applicable to his working hours and accepted that, though frustrating at times, returning late or slipping from his bed in the middle of the night, was par for the course.

Parked on the verge, he waited until West's Defender crept into sight, flashed his headlights, and followed at a snail's pace as they inched their way along the lane to

Baxter's house where the warm, yellow light of a downstairs light spilled onto the drive.

'Glad to see we're not the only ones up,' said West. 'I don't know what I'd do if I had to get them out of bed to break the bad news.'

'Oh, it's never easy, miss, but someone has to do it.'

'That's the worrying thing, me and kid gloves were separated at birth.'

'No bother, you can leave it to me.'

'So, you're used to it?'

'No,' said Duncan, 'you never get used it, but I have done it before, a few times.'

'Oh? How come?'

'As a PC,' said Duncan, 'I had an uncanny knack of drawing the short straw. Doorsteps were my forte. Two fatal collisions, a couple of stabbings, not to mention the odd heart attack here and there.'

'Blimey,' said West, 'you're beginning to sound like a right Jonah. Anyway, thanks for getting here so quick. I had a horrible feeling you'd be over the limit.'

'Well, you were lucky. I was that tired I had my supper and fell straight to my pit.'

'Alright for some,' said West, 'I never made it to mine. Did you get my message?'

'What message?'

'Food.'

'Aye, but everything's shut,' said Duncan, 'you'll have to hang on a wee bit longer, miss.'

'Never mind, maybe I can cadge a biscuit off the Baxters when we go inside.'

'Dougal says you've found the girl.'

'Yup. Stone-cold dead,' said West. 'And it looks like she's got a broken neck.'

'Accident?'

'Not according to McLeod. He seems to think somebody broke it for her.'

'Any ideas?'

'One bloke,' said West. 'He works at the same hotel as Rhona but to be honest we've got absolutely nothing on him, not unless SOCOs find something when they pick his car apart. Shall we?'

* * *

Conscious of the crunch of gravel beneath his boots and wary of spooking the Baxters into believing that an intruder was on the prowl, Duncan stepped lightly and paused beneath the porch.

'So,' he said, as he rapped the door, 'are we keeping quiet about the neck for now?'

'I think so,' said West. 'I mean, I don't know. Let's see how they react. It's one thing telling someone your daughter's dead, telling them you think she was murdered is something else entirely.'

'Who's there?' came a voice from beyond the door. 'Hello? I say, who's there?'

'It's the police, madam. Nothing to worry about.'

West took a step back as a light came on above their heads followed by the sound of a key turning in the lock.

'You gave me a fright,' said Maureen. 'Calling on folk at this time of night. Morning. Whatever it is.'

'Aye, apologies for that,' said Duncan as he flashed his warrant card. 'We've not met but we have spoken to your husband. I'm DS Reid, and this is Detective Inspector West.'

'I see, so you've come with an update on Rhona? Is that it?'

'Aye,' said Duncan. 'A wee update.'

'I'll fetch Willy. He's out back loading feed onto the trailer. You'd best come in.'

Maureen scuttled to the kitchen, yanked open the back door, and called her husband as Duncan and West followed in her wake.

Baxter, wearing the same threadbare sweater and a tweed bunnet atop his head, appeared in the doorway and nodded politely.

'Inspector,' he said. 'Sergeant. Has she offered you anything?'

'No, you're alright,' said Duncan. 'We'll not keep you long.'

'Not even a wee mug of cocoa? It'll see you right.'

'No, thanks all the same.'

'Well, in that case,' said Baxter. 'Let's have it. There's no point in beating about the bush.'

'It's about Rhona,' said West. 'I'm afraid we–'

'For heaven's sake!' said Baxter. 'Of course it's about Rhona! Why else would you be here? So, where was she?'

'Balcreuchan Burn.'

'You mean, she was actually in the water?'

'She was,' said West, hesitating, 'it looks as though…'

'It looks as though she fell,' said Duncan. 'I'm sorry, Willy, Mrs Baxter, but she's not coming back.'

'I see. Well, that's that, then.'

'And I'm afraid there'll have to be a post-mortem. We need to establish the precise cause of death.'

Maureen eased herself into a chair, fumbled in her apron for a tissue, and offered West a vacuous stare.

'I knew something was wrong,' she said as her eyes glazed over. 'But she wouldn't say what. Do you think she was in some kind of bother, perhaps? Do you think it was man trouble, or–'

'We're really not sure,' said Duncan, 'not just now, but we'll do our best to find out.'

'And was she alone?'

'Aye.'

'That's no way to go. Not if you've family, or friends, it's not right.'

'How long?' said Baxter. 'How long will it take for you to chop her up and stitch her back together again?'

'It won't be as brutal as that,' said Duncan. 'I can promise you that, but probably about a week, I imagine.'

'Right,' said Baxter as he turned for the door. 'I've sheep to attend to. They'll not feed themselves.'

'Are you sure?' said West. 'Perhaps you should give yourself a minute, sit down and have a brew. Shock's a funny thing, it can take a while for the news to sink in.'

'I'll cope.'

'And how about you, Mrs Baxter?' said Duncan. 'Are you okay? We can arrange for someone to come sit with you if you're on your own.'

'She'll not be alone,' said Baxter, tersely. 'She has John Barleycorn to keep her company.'

Maureen stood, tucked her chair beneath the table, and opened the sideboard.

'Aye, right enough,' she said, reaching for the bottle. 'If you weren't on duty, I'd offer you a wee drop.'

'That's me away,' said Baxter as he stepped outside. 'You can see yourselves out.'

West took a card from her inside pocket and slid it across the table.

'That's my number, Mrs Baxter. If you fancy a chat, or if you've got any questions, feel free to call, anytime.'

Rankled by the Baxters' stifled reaction to the news of their daughter's demise, West stormed from the house and waited by the car, shooting Duncan a quizzical look as he sauntered up beside her.

'I know what you're thinking,' he said, 'but let's face it, miss, they knew what was coming. They were half-expecting it.'

'Even so,' said West, 'you'd think some show of remorse would be in order.'

Duncan tapped her lightly on the arm and nodded towards the dry stone wall running alongside the house where Willy Baxter sat with his hands on his knees, a lit cigarette dangling from his lower lip.

'Maybe some folk prefer to grieve in private, miss.'

West mustered a sympathetic smile as she strolled towards him.

'You alright, Willy?'

'I thought you'd left,' said Baxter, drawing on his fag.

'We have. I mean, we were just about to. I just thought–'

'What did you think?'

'I was curious,' said West. 'You don't seem that upset considering what's happened.'

'Grief can manifest itself in different ways, Inspector.'

'Yeah I know but, look, I don't want to sound rude, but I can't help thinking there's no love lost between you and your daughter.'

'Oh, nice one, miss,' said Duncan, mumbling under his breath. 'Tactful as ever.'

Baxter took a small, silver tin from his coat pocket, placed the cigarette butt inside, and turned to West, his face erupting in a sea of wrinkles as he frowned and fixed her with a penetrating stare.

'Have you ever been scared, Inspector?'

'Scared? Well, I don't know,' said West. 'Yeah, I suppose so.'

'Have you ever been that scared, that you worry about losing control of your bowels?'

'Oh, aye,' said Duncan. 'Been there.'

'That scared, that you can feel your skin go cold and yet, at the same time, break into a sweat?'

'Well…'

Baxter lowered his voice.

'And do you know what it's like to feel the fear?' he said. 'Real fear? No. I thought not. I'll tell you what it's like, shall I? It's like being told that you have the cancer. It's like being told that you have the cancer at twenty-two years of age.'

'Blimey,' said West, 'that's a bit young.'

'It's too young!' said Baxter. 'But it happened to me!'

'I don't get it,' said West. 'Sorry, but I can't see what you're getting at, and besides, you're still here so–'

'I'm still here because by the grace of God it wasn't my insides ravaged by the disease! It wasn't my liver, or my stomach, or my lungs! It was testicular cancer!'

'Jeez-oh,' said Duncan. 'I'm sorry, pal. Christ, that can't have been easy.'

'See here, Inspector, you want to know what I'm getting at? Well, I'll tell you. There's only one reason I'm still here. It's because they chopped them off. Twenty-two years old and they chopped my baws off. It was the year before we wed, so on you go. You figure it out for yourselves.'

West, suitably admonished, waited until Baxter had disappeared from view then gazed at Duncan, her cheeks billowing with the weight of the sigh.

'Well, that's a turn up for the books,' she said. 'I didn't see that coming.'

'You and me both,' said Duncan. 'You can't help but feel sorry for the fella.'

'So, reading between the lines, what he's actually trying to tell us is that Rhona isn't his daughter after all.'

'Aye, well done, miss. On the ball, as ever.'

'Watch it, you.'

'So, it stands to reason,' said Duncan, 'that Maureen must have known about his condition before they tied the knot.'

'Well, if she didn't, she'd have got a heck of a shock on their wedding night.'

'And Rhona? I'm guessing if they couldn't have bairns of their own, then maybe she was adopted.'

'It's possible,' said West, 'but…'

'But what?'

'Well, if she was adopted,' said West, 'then why does he seem to have such a grudge against her?'

'Families, miss. There could be a hundred reasons. Something as trivial as a personality clash, or maybe she tapped him for a few quid and never paid him back, or maybe she was just a mummy's girl, plain and simple.'

West, eyes wide, grinned at Duncan and slapped him on the shoulder.

'Genius!' she said as she sprinted towards the house. 'I'll get you by the car.'

* * *

Unperturbed by a second knock at the door, Maureen opened it wide and ushered her inside.

'I'd a feeling it was you,' she said. 'Couldn't be anyone else.'

'I'm really sorry,' said West. 'I haven't slept and my head's all over the place.'

'Is it more questions you're after?'

'No, nothing like that. It's my keys,' said West. 'I was fiddling with them earlier and now I can't find the blooming things. I think I might have left them here.'

'Come away through. If they're anywhere, they'd have to be in the kitchen.'

Assisted by a bleary-eyed Maureen, West scoured the table and the worktops, waited until her back was turned, then produced them with a jangle.

'Found them!' she said. 'Thanks again, I'll leave you to get on.'

Jogging back to the car, she reached inside her jacket and surreptitiously handed Duncan a crumpled handkerchief.

'Take this,' she said, 'and follow me.'

'What is it?'

'Maureen Baxter's whisky glass.'

'Are you for real?'

'And you wouldn't?'

'Fair enough. Where are we going?'

'Crosshouse,' said West. 'We're going to get McLeod to do us a huge favour.'

Chapter 15

Like Murdo, the over-inquisitive terrier who stubbornly refused to move from any leaf, lamp post, or fence that held a scent, Munro, having had a sniff of McClusky's reformed lifestyle as an altruistic boat-keeper, could not shake the notion that lurking beneath his humanitarian façade lay the narcissistic sociopath of old.

Niggled by the fact that the avaricious criminal, driven by an obsessive desire to accrue his wealth without the inconvenience of a regular job, was unlikely to realise a sustainable income from the seasonal chartering of a fishing vessel, he pondered the actual source of his revenue as he hastened towards the office, his progress hampered by Murdo's insatiable desire to inspect anything odorous.

Feigning the onset of cramp as a guise to stealthily lift his feet from the floor, Dougal – having spent the entire night fuelled by the findings of forensics, two litres of Irn-Bru, and several packets of dry roasted peanuts – smiled as a jaded Munro drifted through the door with Murdo panting by his side.

'Boss!' he said. 'I thought it was you! Are you up for a brew?'

'I am indeed, aye,' said Munro. 'I brought you some breakfast but I didnae have time to fix myself a cup before we left.'

'How so?'

'I had to attend to several dishes in the West household that Alexander Fleming would have been proud of.'

'So, is she not with you? Westy?'

'No, she isnae,' said Munro, 'but she did have the decency to leave me a note.'

'So, you know about the Baxter girl?'

'Only that they found her,' said Munro as he eased himself into a chair. 'Do you not have any details?'

'All I know is that she was found in the burn. She drowned.'

'Then it's a catastrophe for all concerned,' said Munro. 'Aye, that's the word. Catastrophe.'

'Right enough,' said Dougal. 'Let's hope it was an accident and not...'

'Not what, laddie?'

Dougal handed Munro a mug of hot, sweet tea and helped himself to a bacon roll.

'Well, accidents happen,' he said, 'and by their very definition, boss, they're blameless, but what if it was intentional? What if it was suicide?'

'Suicide?'

'Aye! She may have been depressed. Or on medication. I've read that some of the tablets they hand out these days can turn a normal fella into a–'

'Haud yer wheesht!' said Munro, shaking his head. 'You need to watch your sugar intake, laddie, it's playing havoc with your imagination.'

'I couldn't help it, boss. I needed something to help me concentrate.'

'So, you've been here all night?'

'I have,' said Dougal. 'Amongst other things, I had to charge the Boyd fellas with murder.'

'Then I'm guessing you got the evidence you were after?'

'Oh aye. Forensics nailed them good and proper and just now, I'm finishing up the report for the fiscal, so if it's all the same with you, I need to crack on because I've a feeling when Westy gets back she's going to hit me with a pile of stuff on that Rhona Baxter.'

'So, you've not made any headway on where she went or who she may have seen?'

'Not yet,' said Dougal. 'The only possible link we have is that Callum McClusky, and D&G are still trying to locate him.'

'Good luck with that,' said Munro. 'If he's anything like his father then he's probably halfway to Ulan Bator by now. Right, I'll not disturb you any more, I'll just sit here quietly and look at this computer. Is it switched on?'

'Aye, just lift the lid and away you go. Will I give you a hand?'

'No, you're alright,' said Munro. 'I can take it from here, but if you do find a minute to–'

'Jeez-oh, that's unlikely, boss, for the foreseeable at least.'

'There's no rush, laddie, whenever will do.'

'What is it you're after?'

'Tam McClusky. I'd like to see the state of his accounts, oh, and if he has a registered company for the chartering of that boat of his.'

* * *

Munro, handing Murdo a bite-size morsel of bacon, finished his roll, washed it down with a swig of tea, and donned his glasses, keen to explore the encyclopaedic delights of the internet.

With his index fingers hovering above the keyboard, he carefully typed McClusky's name, checking each letter as it appeared on-screen before proceeding with the next, his efforts punctuated by gasps of frustration at the preemptive text followed by a groan of despair at the proliferation of out-dated articles concerning a heist that had occurred several years earlier.

Disappointed by the lack of relevant results he approached his prey from a different angle, confident that a search for 'Thistledonia' would produce, at the very least, a small nugget of information on the owner, his excitement fading when confronted by the question, '*Did you mean Snowdonia?*' above a series of images relating to a mountainous landscape and the national flower of Scotland.

On the verge of admitting defeat, and deeming the wastepaper basket too small to accommodate the laptop, he removed his glasses and rubbed his eyes before deciding to give the technology one last try by entering the details of McClusky's elusive son.

Surprised to find his name buried in the sub-text of a description hidden amongst the largely irrelevant listings, he followed a link to the Dumfries Academy and in particular, a gallery page dedicated to the school's foreign trips.

Squinting in an effort to focus on the screen, he patiently scoured the captions beneath each image before clicking on one depicting four members of the under-eighteen football team standing on the steps of a hotel in Barcelona, all clearly elated by their outing.

'Dougal,' he said, 'how are you on idioms?'

'Idioms?'

'Aye, you know, popular phrases or sayings like *speak of the devil* or *you cannae judge a book by its cover*.'

'Oh, not bad I suppose,' said Dougal. 'Not that I've ever been tested.'

'Good. Then I think it's time we had a wee quiz.'

'Oh, I'd love to, boss,' said Dougal, grimacing as he rolled his eyes, 'but see here, if I don't finish this report by–'

'Try these for size; *Joined at the…?*'

'Hip.'

'Very good. *As thick as…?*'

'Thieves.'

'And finally; *Invisible threads…?*'

'Make the strongest ties?'

'Full marks, laddie! Now, tell me, what do all these sayings have in common?'

'Oh, I've no idea,' said Dougal, keen to move the conversation on. 'Really, boss, I haven't a scooby.'

'Then I'll leave you with another to ponder while I take wee Murdo for a walk. *If you're looking for something, you'll probably find it…?*'

Irritated by the interruption but unable to stop himself from getting to the bottom of yet another conundrum, Dougal, yielding to his curiosity, marched to the desk and sat before the computer baffled by the banner at the top of the page proclaiming the school's motto 'doctrina promovet' until his eyes finally focused on the text beneath a photograph of the four boys; '*Back of the net for four members of our successful football team. L to R: Davy Allison, Callum McClusky, Paul Riley, Henry Boyd.*'

Scrambling back to his desk with all the finesse of a novice skater in leather-soled shoes, he reached, arms flailing, for his phone and hit speed dial.

'Miss!' he yelled. 'Are you there? Miss! Where are you?'

'Blimey, keep your hair on,' said West. 'We're just getting a coffee.'

'Where?'

'The petrol station, why?'

'I know where Callum McClusky is!'

'About bleeding time,' said West. 'So, Dumfries and Galloway finally managed to–'

'No, no, no!' said Dougal. 'This has nothing to do with D&G. We've the boss to thank for this!'

'Jimbo? What the hell are you… is he there?'

'Aye! No! I mean, he was, he's gone for a walk with the dog!'

'Calm down, for God's sake,' said West. 'Right, deep breaths, slowly now, and… explain.'

'Callum McClusky was at school with Henry Boyd. I think that's where he's hiding. The Boyds' place, in Moffat!'

West, utterly unfazed by Dougal's excitable state, glanced at Duncan, thought for a moment, then spoke with the mundane regularity of a bored customer answering the security questions requested by the bank.

'Right,' she said, 'get on to D&G, tell them to meet us there but listen, not at the house, on the main road, bottom of Star Street, got that? And no noise, understood? Not a peep.'

'Aye, miss, no bother.'

'And if you haven't already, tell DCI Elliot to make the call and smooth things over because if McClusky is there, we're bringing him back to our gaff, no two ways about it.'

* * *

For visitors to the tranquil town of Moffat there were, particularly during the summer, some unexpected sights to behold – amongst them the classic car rally, the country fair, and the annual sheep race where bemused onlookers were able to bet on the knitted jockeys strapped atop the ewes as they bolted through the town. But for the locals there was nothing more peculiar than the sight of four uniformed officers in two patrol cars parked nose to tail outside the Star Hotel, none of whom paid any heed to the dusty Defender hurtling along the High Street, the Audi in hot pursuit, or the occupants who sprinted from the cars and emerged from the butchers three minutes later, each scoffing a cold Scotch pie.

West, dusting pastry from her jacket, stopped opposite the lead car and nudged Duncan in the ribs.

'I don't believe it,' she said despairingly, 'it's flipping smile-a-mile.'

'Sorry?'

'Villiers. What's he doing here? He should be up at the burn.'

'One way to find out.'

'Alright?' said West as they crossed the street. 'What's going on? Moffat's not your patch.'

'I'm under instructions from a DS McCrae to escort the prisoner back to Ayr,' said Villiers. 'That's assuming we have one to transport.'

'Fair enough. Does that mean you've finished up at the burn?'

'Aye, all done, miss. We were there at dawn.'

'And?'

'Nothing.'

'What about SOCOs?'

'Been and gone,' said Villiers.

'Well, did they find anything?'

'No idea. I'm sure they'll be in touch if they have.'

'Give me strength,' said West, gritting her teeth. 'Have you ever heard of a programme called *Curb Your Enthusiasm*?'

'No.'

'Look it up. I think you should audition. Come on.'

Surrounded by the officers at the foot of Star Street, West, in an unprecedented display of leadership, described the location of the house, its corner aspect, and where she wanted three of the four uniforms to position themselves should the suspect attempt an escape via the garage doors or a window on the upper level whilst the fourth, carrying the big key, was armed with the task of gaining entry.

Glancing up and down the street before initiating a countdown with her fingers, she watched as the officer took the antiquated door clean off its hinges before dashing inside only to be confronted by an eerie silence and an empty lounge.

Gesturing towards the door which led to the garage, West waited until Duncan indicated an all-clear before making her way up the stairs to the two double bedrooms where, accepting the etiquette of 'ladies first' as a dying if not out-dated tradition, she willingly stepped aside allowing Duncan, baton drawn, to inspect each of the rooms in turn before pointing to the hatch in the ceiling; the loft, barring the existence of a priest-hole, being the last remaining place a fugitive could hide.

Reaching on tip-toe, Duncan, expanding his repertoire on the subject of short straws, slipped a finger beneath the catch, gave it a tug, and stepped back as the ladder glided gently towards the floor before gingerly making his ascent, aware that a size ten may collide with his head at any moment while West, more than capable of holding her own should a scuffle ensue, followed behind.

Were it not for the combination of dust-balls, mouse droppings, and spiders' webs lining the darkest recesses of the attic then Callum McClusky, secreted behind a manky mattress beneath a decorator's canvas sheet, may have gone unnoticed but the unmistakeable sound of a stifled sneeze, normally deployed by refined members of the upper classes, gave him away.

'A word to the wise, Mr McClusky,' said West, gruffly. 'There's six police officers here, four of whom have Tasers, one of which is pointed directly at your ankles, so if you want my advice, I'd come out now, nice and easy, no sudden movements.'

Apart from the cobwebs dusting his hair and a couple of minor scratches on his arms, McClusky, slithering from the shadows on his belly, looked none the worse for his ordeal.

'That's far enough,' said Duncan as he drew a pair of cuffs from his belt. 'Face down, hands behind your back. Callum McClusky, I'm arresting you under section 1 of the Criminal Justice Act on suspicion of the murder of Miss Rhona Baxter. You are not obliged to say anything but anything you do say will be noted and may be used in evidence. Do you understand?'

Chapter 16

Rewarding Duncan with the facile task of checking McClusky into his budget en-suite accommodation with the proviso that he be left unattended for a couple of hours in the hope that a spell of solitary might exacerbate his desire to co-operate, West, still peckish after what she considered to be a less than satisfying lunch, punched the postcode of Rhona Baxter's address into the sat nav, floored the Defender, and sped towards Stranraer.

United by a morbid fascination for the goings-on at the tiny, detached cottage on Foundry Lane, the neighbours, who barely recognised each other and rarely engaged in conversation, gathered like long-lost friends to hypothesise on the presence of Police Scotland, fielding rumours ranging from a drug-induced break-in to a frenzied knife attack at the hands of a deranged maniac who'd arrived on the late night ferry from Belfast.

Muttering obscenities as she nudged her way through the burgeoning mob of curious bystanders, West, hoping to catch the SOCOs before they left, flashed her warrant card at the uniform on duty, ducked under the cordon, and stepped inside the house which, as Constable Villiers had rightly said, appeared to be awaiting the return of its occupant.

Pausing to catch her breath, she closed the door behind her, snapped on a pair of gloves, and glanced around the lounge, sighing with jealousy when she realised that Rhona Baxter, unlike herself, was something of a clean-freak with a penchant for hoovering.

The only item of furniture, apart from the two-seater sofa, the bookcase, and the glass-topped coffee table, was an oak-veneered sideboard which contained, alongside a stack of old birthday cards and an unused cheque book, a row of box files neatly labelled 'gas', 'electric', 'mobile', and 'bank', the latter of which revealed an incredibly healthy balance on her current account and a credit card statement with an outstanding debt of £36.95 in favour of the Stranraer Tandoori Restaurant.

The kitchen, large enough for the essential appliances but far too cramped for even the smallest of tables, was predictably clean, its showroom appearance marred only by a stained coffee mug on the counter and the faint aroma of something well past its use-by date festering in the bin, whilst the fridge, stocked with a week's worth of food, suggested Miss Baxter had had every intention of returning before it spoiled.

With nothing to the rear of the house but a paved courtyard and a stunning view of Loch Ryan, West – dismissing Baxter's bank balance as nothing unusual for a hard-working professional with little or no time to squander her hard-earned wages – made her way up the narrow staircase.

Pondering the lack of tell-tale clues concerning her disappearance, her train of thought was suddenly interrupted by the unexpected sight of a crouching figure swabbing tiles on the bathroom floor.

'For God's sake!' she said. 'You gave me a fright! I thought I was on my own.'

'So did I,' said the SOCO, glancing over his shoulder.

'DI West.'

'Bob Keane. Are you new?'

'No. Ayrshire.'

'That's why I don't recognise you. So how come you're down here?'

'Because I did something bad in a previous life,' said West. 'Is it just you?'

'Aye, just myself,' said Keane. 'There's no room for more.'

'Fair enough. So, how's it going?'

'Almost there, and if you're in charge, then I've a couple of things that might interest you.'

'I'm all ears.'

Keane placed a hand on the bathtub, hauled himself to his feet, and removed a mask to reveal the battle-weary features of a fifty-two-year-old who, in the course of his work, had aged prematurely.

'Don't take what I say as gospel,' he said, 'you should wait for forensics to confirm–'

'Oh, come on!' said West impatiently. 'Sorry, I don't mean to sound rude, I know you're trying to help me out but I'm up against it here.'

'No need to apologise,' said Keane, 'I know what you lot have to deal with. So, first of all, we've plenty of prints about the place.'

'Is that it? No offence but they're probably all hers, she lived alone.'

'That's as maybe,' said Keane, 'but I can tell you for a fact there's more than one set.'

'You're absolutely sure about that?'

'Positive. And there's traces of blood in the washbasin.'

'No way.'

'Every way. Far be it for me to comment on your investigation, inspector, but if she lived alone, then she certainly didn't cut herself shaving. Not unless she's a contortionist and managed to get her legs up there. No, no. I'd say someone had blood on their hands and they simply rinsed it off. Not washed, mind. Rinsed.'

'Well, how could that happen?' said West. 'Nosebleed, maybe?'

'Maybe,' said Keane, as he flashed her a knowing smile, 'but I'd say it's probably something to do with what was in the toilet bowl, under a wodge of paper.'

'Oh, please!' said West. 'I've just had lunch.'

Keane reached into a brown paper sack and produced a clear plastic bag containing a four-inch, stainless steel paring knife with a wooden handle.

'Not the kind of thing I'd recommend trying to flush down the toilet,' he said. 'Not unless you want to get saddled with a hefty bill from a plumber.'

'And has that–'

'Blood? Aye, it has indeed.'

Given the albeit unconfirmed relationship between Rhona Baxter and Callum McClusky, West, buoyed by the fact that he'd been treated for stab wounds at the Royal Infirmary, smiled as she opened the mirrored cupboard above the basin and eyed the single toothbrush, the dental floss, a packet of panty liners, and a jar of bath salts.

'That's blinding news,' she said, 'thanks, you've just made my day. Have you looked in here?'

'Not yet,' said Keane. 'That's last on my list. I like to finish on my feet, it gets the circulation going again.'

West held the jar aloft and frowned as if examining a specimen suspended in formaldehyde, squinting as the light bounced off its crystalline contents.

'Fancy a wee soak?' said Keane. 'Is that it?'

'Nah, I prefer a shower, me, but…'

'Go on.'

'What about you? Or your missus? Do you use this stuff?'

'Oh, aye,' said Keane. 'Nothing fancy, Epsom salts, mostly. It helps with the joints.'

'Tell me if I'm wrong,' said West, 'but I always thought this stuff was like, well, *chunky*. Like rock salt.'

'Aye, some, but not all. It depends on the brand you buy.'

'Yeah, but this is ultra fine,' said West as she unscrewed the cap, 'I mean, look, it's finer than anything you'd sprinkle on your chips.'

Wary of clogging her lungs with a soothing blend of ylang-ylang or sandalwood, she held the bottle beneath her nose and gently sniffed.

'No fragrance,' she said, as a puzzled look crossed her face. 'I thought the whole point of this stuff was that you stepped out of the bath smelling like a bunch of roses.'

'I wouldn't know,' said Keane. 'I'm not one for perfumes, or aftershave for that matter.'

West tentatively dipped her forefinger into the jar, dabbed it on the tip of her tongue, and smiled as Keane looked on in disgust.

'There must be something wrong with your taste buds if you find that palatable,' he said.

'Oh, but I do!' said West, grinning as she screwed the lid back on. 'And do you know why?'

'Thrill me.'

'Because it's my namesake. *Charlie!* Snow.'

'Cocaine?'

'In one. Bag it, would you, and I need everything you've got sent to FS as soon as possible, can you organise a courier?'

'Aye, no bother.'

'Cheers. Incidentally, how long will it take me to get to the North West Castle Hotel from here?'

'Two minutes,' said Keane. 'Straight up the main road and it's on the right. I'm heading there myself, I've a wee motor car that needs looking at.'

'Perfect!' said West. 'That's me, too. Do you know what you're looking for?'

'Is it woolly fibres you're after?'

'Yup. Passenger seat. Beige colour. I'll meet you there.'

* * *

Unlike the majority of baronial piles scattered about the Scottish landscape, most of which were set in acres of prime woodland, the North West Castle Hotel – a former nineteenth-century country house belonging to the Arctic explorer, Sir John Ross – had long since succumbed to progress and stood isolated in a sea of tarmac bounded by the old port road to the north, an abandoned car park, a sprawling supermarket, and a service station.

Wearing an expression worthy of a left swipe on Tinder, a bamboozled West, confounded by the presence of a class A substance in Rhona Baxter's bathroom, swept up the drive, parked in a secluded spot, and snatched her phone from her hip.

'Dougal,' she said, 'is Duncan with you?'

'He's downstairs, miss, with Callum McClusky. Why? What's up?'

'I think we might be on to something.'

'Oh, aye?'

'Rhona Baxter and Callum McClusky, they were an item, right?'

'No, no. Sorry miss, we *think* they were an item but that's not been proven yet.'

'Okay, let's start again. Baxter had McClusky's number in her phone, right?'

'Correct.'

'And he was the last person she contacted before she disappeared.'

'Okay.'

'And McClusky was treated for stab wounds at the infirmary.'

'Aye, he was,' said Dougal, 'but until we interview him, we'll not know how he–'

'But we do!' said West. 'We just found a knife at Baxter's flat, there's blood on the blade and in the basin, too.'

'So, not a coincidence, then?'

'Not from where I'm standing. And the SOCO's adamant that there's at least two sets of prints about the place. Now, if one set belongs to McClusky then–'

'Then that places him at the scene, miss! Apart from that, it doesn't prove anything at all.'

'What do you know about the power of positive thinking, Dougal?'

'I'd have to say, nothing.'

'Well, I suggest you look into it because I've had enough negativity from Villiers to last a lifetime and I don't think I can take much more.'

'Sorry,' said Dougal, 'I'm coming down off a sugar rush, must be withdrawal symptoms. So, evidence aside, you think Rhona Baxter stabbed Callum McClusky?'

'Hallelujah.'

'Well, it makes sense, I suppose. I mean, maybe that's why she left in such a hurry and spun a yarn to her folks about losing the house.'

'Exactly,' said West. 'Now, moving on, tell me what we know about Rhona Baxter.'

'Successful. Honest. Hard-working. Popular with her pals.'

'Right. So, tell me, what's she doing with a shedload of coke in her bathroom cabinet?'

'Coke? Are you joking me?'

'I kid you not,' said West, 'and when I say shedload, trust me, it's a few grand's worth. So, are you thinking what I'm thinking?'

'I think so,' said Dougal, 'but we're going to need an awful big pen to join these dots.'

'Go on.'

'Okay, Callum McClusky's involved with Rhona Baxter and she has a bottle of coke in her bathroom. McClusky is pals with Henry Boyd who was trafficking cocaine from Iceland to Scotland, on top of which the boat they were using belongs to McClusky's dad, so maybe their relationship was more professional than personal.'

'That's my boy.'

'The only question, then,' said Dougal, 'is why did she stab him?'

'Dunno yet,' said West, 'unless they were mixing business with pleasure. Now listen, the SOCO's sending everything he found up to FS by courier, give it an hour then start chasing them, got it?'

'No bother, miss. What are you up to?'

'I'm at the hotel where Baxter worked. That Dunbar geezer who she used to hang out with should be here by now. We'll see what he's got to say for himself.'

'Okay, have you spoken to Dr McLeod at all?'

'Andy? No, why?'

'He's been asking for you.'

'Probably chasing that drink, I expect. Anything else?'

'Aye, something to cheer you up,' said Dougal.

'God knows I could do with it.'

'I had Kay on the phone, I mean, Miss Grogan.'

'For flips sake, Dougal, I know who your girlfriend is!'

'Sorry. Well, I spoke with Kay and the pellets we found in Henry Boyd's rucksack are the same as those Dr McLeod had, and the DNA from the knife we found with them is his, too.'

'Get in there! So, two knives were used in the attack which means both Jack and Henry Boyd were culpable.'

'*Probably* both culpable.'

'I'll swing for you in a minute. Have you sent that report to the fiscal yet?'

'Aye, miss. All done.'

'Good man,' said West. 'Right, you get yourself off, you've done more than enough. I'll be back about eight, tell Duncan I expect to see him there.'

* * *

West swivelled in her seat and cast an eye over the car park which, being reasonably full despite the time of year, seemed to suggest that the hotel was either a popular destination for one-nighters stepping off the boat, businessmen attending sales conferences, or sports enthusiasts availing themselves of the indoor curling rink but not, unfortunately, the local constabulary conducting a murder inquiry.

Glancing up at the dusky blue sky and a full moon which was guaranteed to send her mood swings into overdrive, West, zipping her coat against an icy blast blowing in off the loch, wandered to the rear of the hotel where, much to her relief, she spied a uniformed officer leaning on the boot of a marked patrol car in an area designated 'staff only'.

'Alright?' she said, waving her warrant card. 'DI West.'

The officer, somewhat startled, looked up, stared for a moment, then walked towards her.

'You're DI West?' he said as a mischievous grin crept across his face.

'Yeah, have you got a problem with that?'

'No, no, I just wasn't expecting… I mean…'

'Don't tell, you thought I'd be some old bloke in a vintage Jag who only listens to classical music.'

'I was about to say, I wasn't expecting anyone so… attractive.'

'Oh, please,' said West, rolling her eyes as she clocked his left hand. 'That ring's on your finger for a reason. And you are?'

'Sergeant Cox.'

'I might have guessed. Right, Alex Dunbar, where is he?'

'In the car. My colleague's trying to coax him out of his shell.'

'What do you mean?'

'He's not budging,' said Cox. 'He's not saying a word unless we arrest him and even then, only through a solicitor.'

'So, what's the problem?'

'Well, what do we arrest him for?'

'For crying out loud!' said West. 'Didn't anyone tell you? Suspicion of abduction and murder.'

'Are you joking me? You mean to say we've been dealing with some kind of nutter?'

'A young lad with a decent job?' said West. 'I doubt it. So, he's keeping schtum, is he?'

'Aye, but to be fair,' said Cox, 'he's not being cocky, or abusive, or violent. If anything, he seems petrified.'

'Right, you wait here, I'll have a word.'

Assuming Dunbar's state of shock to be the result of a predictably intimidating approach by the two uniformed officers, West, preferring to put her suspect at ease rather than scare the living daylights out of him, adopted the kind of flirtatious smile she used to use when frequenting the bars of Shoreditch, leaned towards the open window, and spoke softly.

'Alright?' she said. 'You must be Alex. How's it going?'

Dunbar stared dead ahead and answered succinctly.

'Police?'

'Yeah, I'm a detective. Actually, that's open to debate, but listen, I've been in the car all day long and I could do with stretching my legs. Fancy a walk?'

Dunbar turned to West, swallowed hard, and nodded.

'Just us?'

'Yeah. Once around the car park. How's that?'

'Aye. Okay.'

West opened the door, thrust her hands deep into her pockets, and waited for Dunbar just as Bob Keane, behind the wheel of a small, white Transit van, crept into view.

'Listen, Alex,' she said as they ambled across the tarmac, 'you're not under arrest, and no-one's accusing you of anything, okay? I just need a few words about Rhona.'

'I've nothing to say.'

'I'm sure that's not true, I mean, you work together, right? And from what I hear, the two of you get along famously.'

'So?'

'So all I'm saying is, there's nothing wrong with that. It's not against the law to be mates with a member of the opposite sex. Now, Rhona's not been around much recently, has she?'

'Holidays.'

'Did she go anywhere nice?'

'No idea.'

'So, she didn't send you a postcard?'

'No.'

'When was the last time you saw her?'

Dunbar stopped and stared at West, his face riddled with confusion.

'What's going on here?' he said. 'First, Starsky and Hutch over there, then you. Has something happened to Rhona?'

'I'll tell you later, let's just stick with the question for now. So, when was the last time you saw her?'

'About a month ago.'

'And was that here, at work? Or after?'

'After? What do you mean, after?'

'I hear you and Rhona used to knock about together, is that true?'

'Sometimes.'

'So, what did you do?' said West. 'Go for a few drinks? Was that it?'

'We had an Indian.'

'And after that, did you–'

'Did we what? Listen,' said Dunbar, 'I've no idea what this is all about but I've not done anything wrong, okay?'

'Fine. I believe you,' said West, 'but aren't you worried? I mean, I thought Rhona was due back last week.'

'Aye, she was.'

'And she's not the kind of girl to go AWOL, now, is she?'

'No, she isn't,' said Dunbar. 'Something has happened, hasn't it?'

West, alerted by the sound of an ear-piercing whistle normally reserved for builders hanging off a scaffolding rig thirty feet above street level, turned to see a grinning Keane leaning on the roof of a dilapidated Nissan Micra with his thumb in the air.

'Alright, Alex, listen to me. I don't know where you were going or what you were up to, but I do know that at some point in the last four weeks, Rhona Baxter was in your car.'

'Away! That's tosh!' said Dunbar. 'Why would she be in my car when she only lives up the way.'

West stopped in her tracks, turned to Dunbar, and cocked her head.

'I'm going to let you into a secret,' she said, smiling softly. 'For years I was racked with self-doubt. I spent every single day battling with my confidence, and do you know why? Because my colleagues, my senior colleagues, had no faith in my ability as a cop, which in turn made me wonder if I was in the right job, but you know what? I am. Because despite what they thought, I'm actually quite good at it. I'm quite good at finding stuff out then backing it up with hard evidence. I'll give you an example. The last time you saw Rhona Baxter was about a month ago, right? Well, I can tell you exactly what she was wearing when you saw her – blue jeans, and a beige, woolly sweater. And how do I know she was in your car? Because we just found some beige, woolly fibres on the passenger seat of your motor. So, start talking or I will arrest you and if I do, I'm sorry to say it's not me you'll be dealing with, it's my sergeant, and I'll give you a head's up, he's not a soft touch, not by any stretch of the imagination. It's up to you.'

Unlike the victims of pushy parents who'd cajoled their offspring into believing that education was key to a mortgage-free existence, Alex Dunbar, with one GCSE to his name, had been raised to realise that success did not come from sitting behind a desk, that a hard day's graft was rewarded not with a pay packet but by a sense of achievement, and that the only way to get on was to keep one's head down, respect your elders, and stay out of trouble, an ethos to which he'd strictly adhered and one which, as a consequence of his first encounter with the long arm of the law, had him quaking in his boots.

Shuffling nervously with the pained expression of someone whose bladder was about to burst, he stared at West before throwing his head back and groaning with frustration.

'Oh, Christ!' he said. 'Look, I don't want to get her into trouble, okay? She doesn't deserve it!'

'What do you mean?' said West. 'Get her into trouble?'

'There's a rumour going about the place that she's a boyfriend. The last thing I want is some hulk of a fella giving her a hard time before he comes to batter the hell out of me!'

'Relax,' said West with a reassuring smile. 'I know for a fact that she doesn't have a boyfriend, and she's not married either. So, what was it with you two?'

Dunbar, his shoulders twitching against the cold, glanced needlessly over his shoulder before answering.

'We had a laugh together,' he said, nervously. 'We just got along, okay? Christ knows what she saw in me, I mean, she's nearly old enough to be my mother.'

'And?'

'And one thing led to another. We ended up, you know…'

'Nothing wrong with that,' said West. 'Been there, bought the tee shirt. So, how long were you two seeing each other?'

'I don't know. Six months, maybe.'

'And did anyone else know about your little arrangement?'

'No,' said Dunbar. 'Not that I'm aware of. I mean, the folk at work knew we'd go for a wee bevvy together, but not about the other stuff.'

West proffered a sympathetic smile and lowered her voice.

'Listen, Alex,' she said softly, 'I need to ask you something strictly off the record. I promise you it won't go any further.'

'Is this a trick question?'

'No, I swear I'm being straight, and I hope you will be too. Tell me, was Rhona into drugs at all?'

Dunbar flinched as if he'd been slapped in the face with a wet fish.

'Away!' he said. 'Drugs? Are you joking me? No, no, Rhona's the Mary Poppins of Stranraer! The only drug she ever took was paracetamol, and that was usually for a hangover.'

'And how about you? Are you fond of a smoke? The odd joint? Or anything else, maybe?'

'Not me,' said Dunbar. 'I've never touched the stuff, and I've no intention of starting, either.'

'Glad to hear it,' said West. 'So, back to the car. Where were you going with Rhona?'

Dunbar looked at West and sighed.

'Lendalfoot,' he said. 'Her folks' place. That's where she was going for her holidays.'

'And was that after the Indian?'

'Aye.'

'Tell me something, Alex. Didn't it strike you as odd that she didn't have anything with her? No suitcase, no clothes, no coat, even?'

'No. We left the restaurant and she said she had to go, like she was in a hurry.'

'And where did you drop her?'

'Bottom of the lane, by the main road.'

'So, you didn't go to the house?'

'No.'

'Alright,' said West, nodding towards to the hotel. 'You'd better get a wiggle on or you'll be late for your shift.'

'Is that it? I'm free to go?'

'Yup, just one last thing, I may need to speak to you again, have you got a number?'

'Aye, it's–'

'Hold on.'

West opened 'contacts' on her phone, breathed on the screen, and buffed it on the seat of her pants.

'Here you go,' she said, 'sorry, it's a bit grubby.'

'No danger,' said Dunbar as he tapped away. 'There you go. What about Rhona? Are you going to tell me or not?'

West took a deep breath, looked him in the eye, and sighed.

'I'm afraid Rhona's had an accident,' she said. 'She won't be–'

'Is she dead?'

West nodded.

'Are you okay?'

'Aye.'

'If you want to go home,' said West, 'I can go inside and explain to your boss.'

'No, you're alright,' said Dunbar. 'Best to keep busy. Do they know? In there? Will I tell them?'

'No, you can leave that to me. I'll have a word in a bit.'

* * *

'Are you alright?' said Keane as he walked towards her. 'You look a wee bit, what's the word? *Lost.*'

'I'm fine,' said West. 'Just tired, I think. So, you found the fibres?'

'Aye, beige and woolly, just like you said. Do you know where they came from?'

'We do. Get them up to FS as soon as you can, please, and before you go,' said West as she handed him her phone, 'dust this for me and let me know if you get a decent print, it's the index finger you're looking for.'

Mildly offended that someone should feel the urge to attract her attention by shouting from a distance of less than twenty feet, West turned to see a bemused-looking Cox striding towards her.

'Inspector!' he said. 'Was that not your suspect I just saw walking into the hotel?'

'Yeah, he's late for his shift.'

'Are we not supposed to be bringing him in?'

'Nah, not any more,' said West. 'You can stand down, he's in the clear.'

'Oh. Okay. Well, if you're sure.'

'Yeah, thanks anyway.'

'Some people have no manners,' muttered West as Keane scanned her phone with an FLS. 'Anything?'

'Aye, it's a beauty.'

'Can you lift it? I need my phone back.'

'No bother,' said Keane. 'Just give me a minute.'

'Thanks. The name's Alex Dunbar. I'll need it cross-checked with all the prints you got from Baxter's gaff, and here's my card, give me a bell and hang up so I've got your number.'

Chapter 17

Having swapped the scheming streets of London's vice-ridden Square Mile for a comparatively peaceful existence north of the border, a rejuvenated West – under the sagacious guidance of the now retired DI James Munro – had learned to appreciate the simple things in life like watching the sunrise instead of cowering beneath the sheets, counting the stars instead of pulling the curtains, and sipping a half-decent malt instead of downing half a litre of vodka in less than an hour but there was, without a doubt, no greater pleasure to be had than returning home only to be greeted by a feisty terrier and the welcoming waft of a home-cooked meal emanating from the kitchen.

'If you want a full-time job,' she said, as Munro busied himself with the plates, 'you only have to ask. I should mention, it's a zero hours contract, though.'

'I'm humbled by your generosity.'

'You're looking chipper, what have you been up to?'

'I spent the afternoon in the company of young Dougal,' said Munro, 'and managed to pull myself back from the brink of boredom.'

'Doing what, exactly?'

'I'll tell you when I've dished up.'

'What are we having?'

'One of the butcher's finest pies,' said Munro, 'steak and ale with mashed potatoes and gravy.'

'*You* are one in a million,' said West as she glanced around the kitchen. 'Blimey, where's all the stuff gone?'

'What stuff?'

'The plates, and the pans, and the dishes and stuff.'

'They've been scrubbed to within an inch of their lives and returned to their rightful place in the cupboard.'

'You didn't have to do that.'

'No, I didnae,' said Munro, 'but having spent eleven hours beneath the scalpel of a heart surgeon, I'll be damned if I'm going to run the risk of contracting anything which, at the very least, might play havoc with my digestive system.'

'Oh, don't exaggerate,' said West, 'they weren't that bad.'

'They exceeded the bounds of human decency.'

'Frankly, I don't know what you're worrying about. You could eat a bag of nails and not have any adverse effects.'

'Tell that to the coroner when the death certificate cites Escherichia coli as the cause of death. Now, if you'd be so kind, there's a bottle on the side.'

'Not for me, thanks.'

As someone who'd forged a career out of dealing with death, depravity, and the occasional bag of dismembered body parts, there was little in life capable of shocking James Munro, apart, that is, from the word 'vegan' and his protégé's unprecedented display of temperance.

'Jumping Jehoshaphat! Have you taken a knock to the head?'

'Don't be silly,' said West. 'Callum McClusky's waiting for us. I only nipped back to have some grub before we give him a grilling.'

'Well, kindly refrain from making such ludicrous statements in the future, I'm not sure my heart can take it. Of course, you'll not be offended if I partake?'

'Knock yourself out,' said West. 'Just save some for me, I'll be gagging by the time I get back.'

With Murdo savouring the delights of a ridiculously large ham bone in the lounge, a tactic deployed to stop him begging for scraps, Munro joined West at the table and raised his glass.

'Your very good health,' he said.

'No need to rub it in.'

'So, tell me, Charlie, Jack and Henry Boyd's conviction aside, are you any nearer to finding out who was buying and selling the cocaine aboard the *Thistledonia*?'

'Kind of, why?'

'Because with Dougal's assistance, you'll not be surprised to hear that I'm now of the opinion that Tam McClusky almost certainly has a role in this.'

'You're right,' said West. 'I'm not surprised at all. I was beginning to think the same thing.'

'How so?'

West, jealously eyeing his glass of red, set her cutlery to one side and sipped from a tumbler of water.

'I had a look at Rhona Baxter's bank account,' she said, 'and she's got quite a bit tucked away.'

'Sensible girl.'

'At first I thought, alright, she works hard, she's probably managed to save a bit, but then…'

'I'm listening.'

'But then I got to thinking,' said West, 'somehow or other, she got mixed up with Callum McClusky, right? And he's mates with Henry Boyd. Now, I met a SOCO at her place just now and guess what we found? A stash of coke in the bathroom. So, what if McClusky and Boyd were using her gaff to hide some of their gear, and her bank account to syphon off some of the drug money?'

'It's a reasonable assumption, lassie.'

'Okay, so it stands to reason then that if Boyd was smuggling the drugs from Iceland on Tam McClusky's boat, then he must have known about it. Especially if his son's involved.'

'And I'm inclined to agree,' said Munro. 'Let's not forget, the apple never falls far from the tree.'

'Whatever. The things is, Jimbo, how do we prove it?'

'I'd suggest approaching Tam McClusky from a different angle,' said Munro. 'Snare him by the back door.'

'What?'

'See here, Charlie, Tam McClusky's house in Kirkcudbright was paid for in cash. Of course, that was before the anti money-laundering laws with regard to conveyancing came into force.'

'No offence,' said West, 'but I think we figured that one out already, I mean, he's never worked a day in his life.'

'Aye, but not only that,' said Munro, 'McClusky's been claiming benefits ever since his release from prison.'

'Really? But surely the income from his boat business would preclude him from signing on?'

'Apparently not. According to his annual returns, diligently filed with Revenue and Customs, his profits are well below the six-thousand-pound eligibility threshold, so technically, he's entitled.'

'Entitled my–'

'Plus, he's not working more than twelve hours a week on account of the fact that he cannae walk more than twenty yards without pausing for breath.'

'You mean he's on disability, as well?'

'Aye, emphysema, it seems. So, the question for you, Charlie, is how does someone like Tam McClusky maintain a boat, pay the bills, hand out pay-day loans, and sustain a gambling habit bordering on addiction, on the pittance he earns?'

'And the simple answer to that,' said West, 'is he doesn't. He supplements his income and you and I both know how. My problem is, we don't have enough to arrest him.'

'No, but you do have enough for a warrant. If you can prove financial impropriety then you can hand it over to HMRC, let them do the donkey work. And I wouldnae worry about McClusky, if what I hear is true, then for the sake of appearances, he'll probably welcome you into his home with open arms.'

'Yeah, right, then shoot us in the back as we leave. The thing is, Jimbo, he's not stupid enough to leave anything incriminating lying about his house, but you're right, it's worth a punt.'

'Aye,' said Munro, 'but mark my words, Charlie, do this one by the book, get the warrant before you go knocking his door. He'll not take kindly to being made a fool of. He'll not take kindly at all.'

'Yes, dad. Any pudding?'

'Treacle tart,' said Munro. 'Incidentally, I got your note. Was that not a shock to the system?'

'What?'

'Being up so early.'

'Needs must.'

'You must be shattered.'

'Funnily enough,' said West, 'no. It must be all the adrenalin.'

'So you found the Baxter girl?'

'Yup, face down, in the burn, a mile or two up the road from her parents' house. She drowned.'

'So Dougal said.'

'But not before she had her neck broken. We went to break the bad news to her folks, I had a chat with her old man, it turns out Willy Baxter's a eunuch.'

Munro, wincing as he choked on a forkful of pie, reached for the wine.

'That's not something to joke about,' he said, taking a sip. 'The very thought–'

'I'm not joking,' said West. 'It was cancer. They lopped them off before he got married.'

'So, Rhona Baxter's adopted?'

'Don't know yet,' said West. 'But if she isn't, then her mum's got some explaining to do. McLeod's testing her DNA as we speak.'

'I'm surprised she was willing to give a sample.'

'She didn't,' said West, as she reached for her coat. 'Well, not intentionally, anyway. The glass she was drinking from accidentally fell into my pocket. I need to get a move on, don't wait up.'

Chapter 18

Wrapped in his leather car coat with a woollen watch cap pulled low over his brow and the stubble on his chin bordering on a beard, Duncan, possessing the charm of a nightclub bouncer with a lucrative side-line in knee-capping, fixed Callum McClusky with an unwavering gaze as West, content that her belly was full, placed her phone on the desk and sat with the relaxed demeanour of someone about to binge on a box set of *Sex and the City* before shattering the silence by reaching forward and clicking the button on the voice recorder.

'The time,' she said softly, 'is 8.17pm. I'm Detective Inspector West, also present is Detective Sergeant Reid. For the benefit of the tape, would you please state your name.'

'Callum.'

'Your full name.'

'McClusky.'

'Do you know why you're here, Callum?'

McClusky, the rings under his eyes exaggerated by the ghostly pallor of his pale, blotchy skin, thought for a moment and smiled.

'Breaking and entering.'

'Wrong answer,' said West. 'There were no signs of a forced entry at the premises on Star Street, so to arrest you on suspicion of such would have been foolish on our part. Would you care to try again?'

Suffering from a lack of sleep and missing the comforts of home, McClusky, slouching in his seat with his legs splayed, opted to heed his father's advice and, having declined the offer of a phone call and the services of a solicitor, decided to speak only when spoken to, and to keep his answers to the bare minimum.

'No,' he said.

'Then I suggest you try your hand at some memory games,' said West. 'I'll remind you. You were arrested on suspicion of murder. Have you anything to say about that?'

'No.'

'Good. If we carry on like this, I might get an early night, and God knows I could do with one. How long have you known Henry Boyd?'

McClusky shuffled in his seat and blinked nervously.

'No comment.'

'Well, you must know him pretty well,' said West. 'After all, you were in his house. How'd you get in? Do you have a key?'

'No comment.'

'You were at school together, weren't you? Do you hang out a lot, you and Henry? Go for a few pints, watch the football, maybe?'

'No comment.'

Having interviewed enough young offenders to know when someone had been advised to answer any questions with the volition of a seasoned pro, West, going out on a limb, decided to embellish the facts in an effort to rattle his cage.

'I think it's a shame you don't want to talk about him,' she said, 'because he speaks highly of you. He says you see each other quite a lot. In fact, he even said you have a right laugh together, especially on the boat. Your old man's boat. The *Thistledonia*.'

McClusky glanced at West, raised his eyebrows, and smirked.

'Jack and Henry are quite fond of fishing, aren't they?' said West. 'They go quite regularly. How about you, Callum? Do you like fishing?'

'No comment.'

'Well, you must like it a little bit, I mean, that's what you do for a living, isn't it? Flogging fish off the harbour.'

'No comment.'

'Henry tells me they go all the way up to the Faroes. Not far from Iceland, is it? The Faroes. Do you know anyone from Iceland?'

'No comment.'

'Jack does,' said West. 'They know a geezer called Aron. Or should I say, *used to know* a geezer called Aron. He's dead now. Drugs. That's what killed him. Are you into drugs, Callum?'

'No comment.'

'What about your dad?' said West. 'I mean, I know he's getting on a bit but he strikes me as the kind of bloke who'd get a kick from chasing the odd dragon about the place.'

Unnerved by Duncan's protracted silence, McClusky shook his head and watched as West, looking as bored as an Amish electrician, checked her watch, placed her elbows on the table, and cradled her head in her hands.

'How long have you known Rhona?' she said with a sigh. 'Miss Rhona Baxter.'

'Never heard of her.'

'Sorry, weren't you meant to say "no comment" there?'

'I said, I've never heard of her.'

'Then why does she have your number in her phone?'

'*No comment*.'

'That's more like it. Rhona wasn't into drugs, was she? She was a sensible girl, a career girl. Hard-working, honest, decent. Which makes me wonder why she had a jar of cocaine in her house. I'd say that was odd, wouldn't you?'

'No comment.'

'The thing is, Callum, Rhona's dead too. Only her death had nothing to do with drugs. Somebody snapped her neck in half and left her to drown in the burn.'

McClusky, the colour draining from his cheeks, glanced furtively about the room, cleared his throat, and lowered his gaze.

'What makes it worse,' said West, 'is that she was still alive when she hit the water but she couldn't move. You see, the break in her neck severed the spinal cord, which paralysed her, so she lay there for hours, slowly drowning and freezing to death, and there was nothing she could do, but wait. I'll ask you again, Callum, when was the last time you saw Rhona Baxter?'

'No comment.'

McClusky snatched his hands from his pockets in an effort to stop himself falling from his seat as the unexpected sound of Duncan's fist thumping the desk sent him reeling to one side.

'For God's sake!' he said, getting to his feet. 'I've met parrots with a better vocabulary than you! See here, McClusky, ordinarily I'm a very patient fella but the thing with me is, if I've not had my sleep, and if I've not had my supper, I get irritable, and when my fuse is burnt, I get angry! Do you get what I'm saying?'

With his right leg succumbing to an involuntary twitch, Callum McClusky, his eyes misting over, gripped the sides of the chair and slowly slid back in his seat.

'You!' said Duncan, as he walked towards him. 'You're just like the rest of them! Out there, on the street, you think you're something special, you think you're the big man, but one whiff of a spell in the big house with the wee windows and you start bleating like a wean. Well, I've got some news for you, pal, you'd best buy yourself a big box of tissues because that's exactly where you're going, with the rest of your pals.'

'How?' said McClusky, trying to muster some courage. 'You can't put me away for not answering your questions.'

'I'm not bothered about the questions!' said Duncan. 'As far as I'm concerned, they're just a formality. You're going down for the murder of Rhona Baxter.'

'I didn't do it!' said McClusky, wiping his eyes. 'And you can't prove that I did!'

'Aye, we can!' said Duncan, as he made for the door. 'And when you get out, you'll be an old man! For the benefit of the tape, DS Reid has left the room.'

West looked at McClusky and raised her eyebrows.

'Now you've done it,' she said. 'Interview suspended. The time is 8.53pm. I've had enough too. I'm going home.'

Alone with West, McClusky, reverting to form, stared across the room with a contemptuous grin smeared across his face.

'What's up?' he said. 'Can you not handle an interview without some meathead to back you up?'

'Tread carefully,' said West. 'You've no idea who you're dealing with.'

'Look at me, I'm quaking. So, if you're off, is that me away, too? Am I free to go?'

'You must think I'm zipped up the back, you muppet. The only place you're going, is back in your box.'

'You can't do that!' said McClusky. 'If you're not charging me, then you have to let me go.'

'Listen, sunshine. I can hold you for twelve hours, and if your grasp of the English language hasn't improved by then, then I can hold you for another twelve, so if I were you, I'd get some kip. Night, night.'

* * *

There were only three occasions in her entire life when DI Charlotte West, witnessing the hitherto unseen dark side of an individual's character, had been left in a state of confused shock.

The first, as a young teen, was when her animal-loving riding instructor dispatched a defenceless mouse with the heel of her boot. The second, instigated by an excess of alcohol, was when her otherwise kind, caring, and loving ex-fiancé threatened to send her into orbit with a single jab from his right hand, whilst the third, a masterclass in interview techniques, was watching a menacing DI James Munro turn a cold-blooded killer into a quivering wreck with nothing more than a few choice words delivered with the softly-spoken but chilling conviction of a lifer in Broadmoor.

Duncan Reid, waiting patiently on the stairwell, had slipped in at number four.

'Have you calmed down?' said West as she trudged towards him.

'Sorry?'

'I never realised you had such a temper, damn near scared the pants off me.'

'Oh, that's not a temper, miss. That was all an act.'

'See you at the BAFTAs, then.'

'See here, miss, I grew up with the likes of McClusky, they're all mouth and no trousers, the reason being, they think they can get away with it because a decent brief and a social worker will claim they're victims of society and a deprived childhood. It's all tosh as far as I'm concerned, putting a rocket up their backside doesn't do them any harm.'

'Well, I think you managed to get Apollo 12 up his.'

'Call me the harbinger of doom,' said Duncan, 'but he does have a point.'

'What are you on about?'

'Rhona Baxter, miss. We can't prove it was him.'

'That's a minor inconvenience for now,' said West. 'You have to learn to trust fate, Duncan. Something will turn up.'

'I'm not sure it's fate we're needing, miss. It's divine intervention.'

Noticing the chink of light glowing beneath the office door, West, assuming Dougal had failed to follow her instructions to go home and get some rest, swung it open only to find the willowy Dr McLeod seated at her desk watching an episode of *Quincy* on Netflix.

'Andy!' she said. 'What the hell are you doing here?'

'Well, if the mountain won't go to Mohammad.'

'Excuse me?'

'I left a message,' said McLeod. 'Several, in fact.'

'Yeah, sorry about that, it's been the longest day.'

'For all of us.'

'You're not wrong there,' said Duncan. 'I'd offer you a drink but as you're driving the choice is limited to tea, coffee, or Dougal's Irn-Bru.'

'You're alright,' said McLeod. 'I'm not stopping now that you're here.'

'You are silly,' said West. 'Surely it could have waited.'

'I'm afraid not, Charlie. I'm rammed solid from 5am and I thought I should tell you to your face.'

'Is this about Baxter?'

'Aye, which one do you want?'

'How many have you got?'

'Two,' said McLeod. 'Rhona and Maureen.'

'Let's start with Rhona. She's the hot topic at the moment.'

'Okay, well, you'll be pleased to know, it's as I thought. It's not just the second vertebra in her neck, the C2, that was fractured, the C1 was out of alignment and the C3 had a fracture, too.'

'Meaning?'

'Meaning that the vertebral arteries were ruptured which resulted in a lack of blood to the brain. That, coupled with the damage to the cervical nerves, left her paralysed. So it's like I said, she drowned.'

'What a lovely note to end the day on.'

'I'm not finished yet,' said McLeod. 'On the upside, I retrieved some skin tissue and a few strands of hair from beneath her fingernails…'

'Which means,' said Duncan, 'that she must have been involved in some kind of a tussle?'

'Exactly. The DNA confirms that both samples come from the same person. The profile's on the system but there's no match.'

'Not yet, there isn't,' said Duncan, 'but there soon will be.'

'Oh?'

'Our prime suspect is downstairs. His details should be up by the morning and I reckon he's the man.'

'Do you know what?' said West. 'If I wasn't so flipping tired, Andy, I'd buy you that drink. Right now.'

'Rain check, Charlie, but I will hold you to it. Now, will I give you the story on Maureen?'

'Christ, I'd almost forgotten about her,' said West. 'Yeah, go on.'

'Okay, you were of the opinion that her daughter was adopted, is that not right?'

'Well, it's a theory,' said West, 'seeing as how her husband lost his battle with testicular cancer.'

'Battle?'

'Yup, but it's okay, he won the war.'

'I'm glad to hear it,' said McLeod, 'but I'm afraid it's back to the drawing board as far as your theory's concerned. The DNA from the glass you gave me proves that Maureen Baxter is definitely Rhona's mother.'

'Oh dear,' said Duncan. 'I'm not sure if that's good news or bad.'

'How so?'

'Because now we need to find out who the father is, and it's not something I'm keen on discussing with a man who can't have kids.'

Chapter 19

Likening the course of an investigation to a trudge through the mire requiring the dogged determination of Pheidippides racing to Athens, Munro – intent on finding a link between the class A substance in Rhona Baxter's bathroom and Tam McClusky's uncanny ability to evade detection by both Revenue and Customs and the Department for Work and Pensions – commandeered a laptop and, wallowing in the serenity of the empty office, instigated a search of the National Records of Scotland while Murdo, unfazed by the ungodly hour, chomped his way through a bowlful of breakfast.

Handling the keyboard with the tenacity of a bomb-disposal expert assessing an IED, he smiled with relief when, after the minimum of effort, the NRS homepage appeared, his elation evaporating as he realised the website had been designed by the person responsible for the maze at Hampton Court Palace until, by chance, he happened across a link to 'Scotland's People' where a surprisingly simple search of the marriage records brought forth a cornucopia of unexpected results.

‘Boss!’ said Dougal, side-stepping Murdo as he careered through the door. ‘Jeez-oh! I didn’t expect to find you here! In fact, I wasn’t expecting anyone at all!’

‘Milk and three, if you’d be so kind,’ said Munro as he removed his spectacles. ‘I’m parched.’

‘Coming up! Have you not had yourself some breakfast?’

‘No, wee Murdo’s scoffed the lot.’

‘Then here, have mine,’ said Dougal as he handed him a sausage sandwich, ‘I can wait. Duncan will bring supplies soon enough.’

‘I’m indebted, laddie. Truly, I am.’

‘No bother, it’s the least I can do. So, what brings you here so early? Did you not sleep?’

‘I slept very well,’ said Munro, ‘but that Tam McClusky’s been getting under my skin.’

‘How so?’

‘His financial shenanigans for a start, not to mention that blessed boat of his. To his credit though, he’s old school, he knows how to cover his tracks, I’ll give him that.’

‘Aye, you’re not wrong there,’ said Dougal. ‘So, are you looking for ways to trip him up?’

‘I am.’

‘Good luck with that. We’ve tried but there’s not much on him.’

‘Where did you look?’

‘The usual,’ said Dougal, ‘council records, and HMRC as you said, but to be honest, as he’s not in the frame for anything, I didn’t dig too deep. He seems to have kept his nose clean since he got out of jail.’

Munro finished his sandwich, took a swig of tea, and proffered his cup for a refill.

‘I’ll give you a wee tip,’ he said. ‘If you ever have to deal with the likes of McClusky again, then dinnae waste time looking at the present or what he might do in the future. You need to go back. Way back.’

'Oh?'

'Are you familiar with the phrase "the past will always come back to haunt you"?'

'I am, aye.'

'Well, I've just found McClusky's ghost.'

* * *

West, wearing the look of a distraught mother who'd finally found her itinerant child, hovered in the doorway and rolled her eyes.

'There you are!' she said. 'So, what's this? Tit for tat?'

'I'm not with you, Charlie?'

'Leaving me a note then skedaddling while I was still asleep!'

'Not intentional, lassie. I had something on my mind.'

'Now, now,' said Duncan, grinning as he plopped a bagful of food on the desk, 'if you're going to argue, take it outside. Chief, how's it hanging?'

'Very well,' said Munro. 'I take it you're suitably rested?'

'I certainly am, but why are you out of your pit so early?'

'I've been looking for a length of rope.'

'Sorry, chief, too early for riddles.'

'For McClusky to hang himself.'

West draped her jacket over the back of a chair and helped herself to a fried egg sandwich as Dougal served tea.

'Carry on like this,' she said, 'and you'll be headhunted by Oxfam.'

'I'm not with you, Charlie.'

'They'd kill to get a volunteer like you.'

'Very good,' said Munro, 'but my role as an unpaid domestic is time consuming enough.'

'Touché. Okay, let's have it, I'm looking forward to this.'

Munro stood, grabbed his tea, and wandered to the window with one hand firmly behind his back.

'Okay,' he said, gazing at the street below, 'Tam McClusky. Did you know his parents were born in Londonderry?'

'That'll explain his love of firearms,' said Duncan.

'And did you know his wife, Kelly McClusky, née Fraser, is now running a souvenir shop in Stirling?'

'Business must be good,' said Dougal, opening his emails, 'if she can afford to live up there.'

'And did you know that Tam McClusky and Kelly Fraser were wed at the registration office on Buccleuch Street in Dumfries?'

'Always fancied a white wedding myself,' said West, 'but heigh-ho. So, where exactly are you going with all this?'

'The witness at the ceremony,' said Munro, 'was one Maureen Hughes who, just two months later, went on to marry a certain William John Baxter.'

'Bloody hell!' said West, spluttering into her tea. 'So, they know each other! That's a bit bleeding close for comfort, isn't it?'

Munro, an advocate of fidelity and a believer in the sanctity of marriage, returned to his seat, narked by his own theory.

'You said McClusky divorced because of some life-changing circumstances, is that right?'

'Well, that's what he told me,' said West. 'Frankly, it's hardly surprising, I mean, if he went down for armed robbery then his missus probably didn't like the idea of being labelled a gangster's moll. Why do you ask?'

'Because I'm not convinced that that's the reason at all. In fact, I'm of the opinion that Tam McClusky and Maureen Baxter had, what shall we call it? An arrangement. Aye, that's the word, an arrangement.'

'Oh, come off it!' said West. 'Surely you're not suggesting they've been at it all these years!'

'Perhaps not as long as that,' said Munro, 'but early on, around the time of the wedding, aye, I'd wager they were.

You yourself said William Baxter was incapable of siring any offspring.'

'Yeah, but…'

'Then where did Rhona Baxter come from? And before you answer, I'll have you know I'm not a fan of gooseberries, and storks are indigenous to tropical Asia and sub-Saharan Africa only.'

'Thank you, David Attenborough. Alright, Jimbo, we'll put your theory to the test, it's easily done. McClusky's got form, his DNA's on the database, we'll simply run a cross-check with Rhona's.'

'I'll do it,' said Dougal, 'you can leave it with me.'

'Speaking of McClusky, we need to get going. Have we got that warrant sorted?'

'Aye,' said Dougal, 'it's right here, but can I ask, should we not be trying to establish a link between McClusky and the Boyds instead of going after his finances?'

'With any luck,' said West, 'that's exactly how we'll establish a link. Now, anything else before we push off?'

'Aye, I've an email here from Dr McLeod sent at 4.37 this morning.'

'Good God, poor bugger gets less sleep than us.'

'The hair and tissue samples from Rhona Baxter's fingernails are a match positive for Callum McClusky.'

'Right, that's me away!' said Duncan. 'It's time I had another word with that wee windbag. Do we have enough to charge him?'

'Whoa! Hold your horses!' said West. 'Not so hasty, we've plenty of time yet. Let's get an ID on the prints from her bathroom first, plus, we need to find out where his little fish van is; it's the only way he could've got to the burn and we need to prove Rhona was with him. We can ask his dad when we get there. Dougal, can you sort a car to bring him back?'

'Aye, no bother,' said Dougal, 'but are you not forgetting something?'

'Don't think so, why?'

'Tam McClusky's in Dumfriesshire.'

'I know. Kirkcudbright. What's that got to do with… oh, crap! You'd better make another call, get The Bear out of bed if you have to but do it now, we can't–'

'Charlie!' said Munro. 'Listen to yourself!'

'What?'

'All you're doing is complicating matters. McClusky, is he aware that young Callum's in a cell?'

'No.'

'Then when you get there, tell him his son's been arrested and he's been asking for him. Offer to bring him back here, and once he's downstairs you can arrest him on suspicion of art and part.'

'Is that allowed?'

'Probably. Well, as long as Duncan finds something in his house by the time you get back.'

* * *

Since ditching the aesthetically pleasing but woefully inadequate Nissan Figaro for something altogether more practical, West, deriding anything called a 'sportback' as fodder for petrolheads and boy-racers, had quietly conceded on several occasions that the Audi, whilst not entirely suited for powering up a hillside in six inches of snow, was undoubtedly more comfortable than her ageing Defender.

Succumbing to the soporific effect of the sprung seats and hyper-efficient heating system, she finally managed to rouse herself from her somnolent state and delighted in taunting Duncan for his lack of special awareness as they arrived at McClusky's house.

'And you had the cheek to have a pop at me!' she said as the heavens unleashed another deluge. 'Move forward, you're taking up the space of two cars!'

'We're okay here,' said Duncan, smarting as a bolt of lightning flashed across the sky. 'That's not going to clear anytime soon.'

'I should've bought a bleeding houseboat,' said West. 'What's the forecast? Any sunshine on the way?'

'No, no. That's us till summer, miss.'

'Very funny.'

'I'm not joking,' said Duncan. 'As Billy Connolly once said, Scotland has two seasons, June and winter. So, any plans for the weekend?'

'If we're not working, you mean? No. Not yet. You?'

'Well, a couple of years ago I'd have been looking forward to getting blootered after the match but these days it's all about making sure the wellies are clean and the sandwiches are packed. I'll no doubt be off on another trek with Cathy and the wean.'

'You're mellowing before your time,' said West, 'but in a good way.'

'Happens to us all,' said Duncan. 'You should give that Dr McLeod a bell, invite him over for Sunday lunch. It'll do him good to carve something other than a body.'

'Yeah, maybe,' said West. 'I'll see what Jimbo's up to first. I can't bear the thought of him being on his own.'

'Aye, I get that, but he's not on his own, he's got Murdo.'

'That's what worries me. I'm frightened that mutt will walk him to an early grave.'

'So, will we mention the warrant?'

'Nah, not unless we have to,' said West. 'Let's see if he comes quietly first. You can slip in once we've gone. Oh, and don't waste time trying to figure out what he had for breakfast, it's financial stuff we're after.'

'Roger that.'

'Incidentally, how are you going to get in? No lock-picking allowed.'

Duncan reached into his pocket and produced a set of keys.

'Callum McClusky's,' he said, jangling them in front of her. 'He'll not be needing them for a while.'

'Crafty bugger,' said West as Duncan, one eye on the rear-view mirror, fired up the Audi and crept forward, allowing just enough room for a marked patrol car to park behind. 'Smartarse, too. Right, let's hope he's in.'

* * *

The front door, as seemed to be the norm, was swinging on its hinges, the occupant, wherever he was, clearly untroubled by the wind howling down the hall.

'Anyone home?' yelled West as she rapped on the door.

'I'm in the office! Come away through!'

Expecting to find McClusky seated behind an executive desk surrounded by shelves of neatly organised files, West, shaking the rain from her hair, was surprised to find that the office was, in fact, a vintage drop-leaf bureau cluttered with crumb-laden plates, empty coffee mugs, and discarded copies of the *Racing Post*, wedged in the alcove of the living room where McClusky, hastily closing all of the drawers, was struggling to free himself from the arms of an antique Windsor chair.

'Inspector! Sergeant! You should've called ahead, I'd have put the kettle on!'

'I hope we're not interrupting,' said West. 'We could wait if you're busy.'

'Not at all! I'm just catching up on some paperwork, totting-up how much I've lost through cancelled bookings.'

'No computer?'

'Computer?'

'For all your spreadsheets and stuff.'

'I've no idea what you're talking about,' said McClusky, waving a blue, hardback book. 'I use a ledger. Every transaction entered in ink by my own fair hand. Still no news on the *Thistledonia*, then?'

'I'm afraid not,' said Duncan. 'Maybe the insurance could help you out, you know, with loss of earnings and the like.'

'Oh, they'll not be bothered with that, Sergeant, just the damage to the boat and believe me, once the loss adjuster's taken a look, I'll still not get what's due. Is there no way of speeding things up a wee bit? I need to get her back in the water as soon as possible.'

'I'll try,' said West, 'but just out of curiosity, why the rush? I mean, who'd want to sail the seven seas at this time of year?'

'You'd be surprised,' said McClusky, 'there's plenty a fool willing to part with their cash for a glimpse of Davy Jones's locker.'

'If you say so.'

'Now, will I get you that drink? What's it to be? Tea or coffee?'

'No, you're alright,' said Duncan, 'we're not stopping.'

'As you wish. So, to what do I owe the pleasure?'

'We were wondering if Callum had left his car here.'

'You came all the way here to ask me that?'

'Amongst other things, aye.'

'It's at the bottom of the drive,' said McClusky, 'and it's not moved in days.'

'Mind if we take a look?'

'What for?'

'Nothing important.'

'Here,' said McClusky as he tossed them the keys. 'Be sure to lock it when you're done. Heaven knows where the lad's got to.'

West leaned against the door, slipped her hands into her pockets, and smiled.

'He's feeling better then, is he?'

'Sorry?'

'Callum. The flu.'

'Oh aye, the flu! Aye, much better, it's kind of you to ask.'

'No worries,' said West, 'although I have to say, he's still looking a bit peaky.'

'Peaky? So you've seen him?'

'Yup. Several times. He's been asking for you.'

'Well, where on earth is he?'

'He's at our place. In a cell. He's been arrested.'

McClusky wrestled himself from the confines of the chair, ran his fingers through his thick, grey locks, and scratched the back of his head.

'Sorry,' he said with a frown. 'I'm confused, Inspector. Arrested? What for?'

'Long story,' said West. 'I'll tell you on the way. So, do you want to see him or not?'

As an experienced con well-versed in the underhand tactics of the local constabulary, Tam McClusky, unsettled by the fact that two detectives had travelled sixty odd miles to simply offer him a lift, was wily enough to spot a ruse when he saw one but concluded, nonetheless, that to decline such an offer, would only arouse their suspicion.

'I suppose I better had,' he said. 'I'll fetch my coat. Just one thing, Inspector, if he's been arrested, then why did he not phone?'

'Dunno,' said West, 'but if it's any consolation, he refused a brief as well. You can ask him when we get there.'

* * *

West, waiting by the patrol car, seized the opportunity to make a discreet call while McClusky, fumbling with his keys, double-locked the front door.

'Are you not coming, Sergeant?'

'I am,' said Duncan, 'but I need a wee peek at Callum's motor first. I'll be along shortly, don't you worry.'

Unperturbed by the relentless downpour, Duncan, ambling along the drive like a pensioner out for a Sunday stroll, waited until they'd slipped from view before turning on his heels and dashing back to the house where he began his search by leafing through the ledger McClusky had proudly displayed moments earlier before discarding it, on the grounds that they'd require the services of a graphologist to decipher the handwriting.

Faring no better as he poked around the pigeonholes, which, belying their intended use as a receptacle for mail, messages, and memoranda, had been stuffed with an assortment of cobweb-coated snacks and savouries – including a half-eaten Tunnock's teacake, a stale packet of fig rolls, and several empty crisp packets – he turned his attention to the row of six drawers and, working left to right, began systematically sifting his way through each in turn when, frustrated at finding nothing more than a raft of receipts, used betting slips, and a bundle of IOUs from needy neighbours, he froze with his hand on the fifth, unnerved by a hefty bang on the door.

Wielding his warrant card to ward off anyone brave enough to question the presence of an unshaven scruff in McClusky's house, he yanked it open and gazed quizzically at a weary-looking gent toting an aluminium attaché case.

'Bob Keane,' he said. 'Your DI just called.'

'Sorry?'

'Scenes of crimes.'

'Oh, smashing!' said Duncan as he handed him the key. 'It's a wee white van at the bottom of the drive. Did she tell you what to look for?'

'Aye, same as before.'

'Well, on you go. Give me a shout when you're done.'

With his expectations of finding anything incriminating dwindling at a rate of knots, Duncan, his patience wearing thin, returned to the office, opened the fifth drawer and, retrieving three sets of keys, began to wonder if McClusky, not one to declare his business interests, was running a letting agency on the side.

Dismissing them as spares for the house, the garage, and possibly Callum's car, he tossed them back in the drawer, dropped to his knees and opened the double doors to the cupboard beneath where, dismayed at the amount of tat one man could hoard, he began ferreting through the contents of two large shoeboxes containing a variety of Christmas baubles, a string of fairy lights, and a handful of leaking batteries before opening each and every case of a ridiculously large collection of antiquated VHS cassettes, his efforts interrupted by the sound of Bob Keane hollering from the hallway.

'That's me,' he said. 'I'll leave you to it.'

'No danger,' said Duncan, 'did you get what we need?'

'Aye, fluff off the seat. I'd say it's the same as the fibres I got from the other fella's car. I'll send them to FS for confirmation.'

'Magic! I'll give Westy a bell and let her know. Anything else?'

'Only this,' said Keane, waving a plastic pouch. 'It's a wee piece of upholstery from a tear in the seat.'

'Will we get anything off it?'

'Don't hold your breath,' said Keane, 'it's worth a shot but to be honest I reckon the only thing FS will tell you is that it came from a Volkswagen.'

Returning to the bureau, Duncan, confounded by the fact that neither the boxes nor the tapes would fit back inside the cupboard, paused as the word 'Volkswagen' rang in his ears, leapt to his feet, and took the car key from the drawer.

Baffled by the Toyota logo on the fob, he reached for the other sets, laid them side by side and, frowning as if trying to solve another of Munro's cryptic conundrums, stared at the lucky rabbit's foot on one, and the red, Spanish beer logo on the other.

'Oh, you dancer!' he said, grinning as the penny dropped.

Trying his best to contain his excitement, he pulled open the sixth drawer and, his mood lifted by the sight of two padded brown envelopes, stuffed everything into his pockets, raced outside, and fired up the Audi.

'Dougal!' he said, yelling at the phone as he skidded down the street. 'Is Westy back yet?'

'Not yet, pal. What's the story?'

'Tell her she's to arrest McClusky, then do nothing till I get back, have you got that? Do nothing till I get back!'

Chapter 20

Relying on instinct rather than cold, hard facts, Munro – blessed with the patience of a saint – was used to stalking his prey with the steadfast resolve of a grand master in a title tournament whilst Dougal, cut from the same cloth, displayed the composure of a sated sloth as he waited for the trout to bite, whereas West, irascible by nature, would snap at the slightest hint of a delay to her schedule, especially if Uber Eats were involved.

'What's keeping him?' she said, pacing the floor. 'He should've been here by now!'

'All good things come to those who wait,' said Munro, sarcastically.

'He's right,' said Dougal. 'Some things in life are worth–'

'Oh, shut up, the pair of you! This is doing my nut in!'

'Well, I suggest we do something to take your mind off matters,' said Munro. 'A wee game perhaps. I spy with my little eye–'

'I don't believe I'm hearing this.'

'–something beginning with "L".'

'Well, it's definitely not lunch.'

'It's lamp. Dougal, your turn.'

'I spy with my little eye something beginning with "T".'

'Good idea,' said West. 'Stick the kettle on.'

'It's terrier, miss.'

'It'll be traction if you don't pack it in.'

'Are you lot arguing again?' said Duncan, grinning as he barged through the door. 'You're like a bunch of weans!'

'Where have you been?'

'As the chief would say, I went to fetch some nails.'

'What?'

'For somebody's coffin. Did you not get my message? Have you arrested McClusky?'

'Yes I have! And by the way,' said West, 'you'll be pleased to know Jimbo was right.'

'No change there, then. Right about what, exactly?'

'Tam McClusky,' said West. 'He's Rhona's father.'

'Dear, dear, and I thought I had a chequered past.'

'On the downside, though, the prints in her bathroom belong to her and Alex Dunbar. Not a single set belong to Callum but the DNA on the blade does.'

'Which proves he was stabbed in her bathroom. So, prints aside, do we have enough to charge him?'

'Almost,' said West. 'All we need to prove now is that she was with him in his car.'

'Job done,' said Duncan. 'Your pal, Keane, the SOCO, he got some fibres off the passenger seat. He reckons they're the same as the ones he lifted from Dunbar's motor.'

'Yes! Back of the net!' said West, punching the air. 'Right, listen up, we know he was involved with Rhona Baxter, we've got fibres from her sweater in his car, and we've got his hair and tissue samples from beneath her fingernails. On top of that, he still refuses to tell us where he was on the night she disappeared, so I say we go ahead and charge him. Anyone say otherwise?'

'No, no. I'd say you're on the money there,' said Duncan. 'Besides, the clock's ticking, we need to do it soon.'

'Good. Dougal, you do the honours. Nip downstairs then get cracking on the report for the fiscal.'

'Aye, aye, miss.'

'What about Alex Dunbar?' said Duncan. 'Is he on his way in?'

'No,' said West. 'I've thought the better of it. He's not the strongest of characters, if we give him the once over here it'll probably break him in two, so I'll drive over later and have a friendly word in his shell-like.'

'But if he stabbed Callum McClusky,' said Dougal, 'then should we not do him for ABH?'

'We'd need McClusky to press charges for that,' said West, 'and frankly, I can't see that happening anytime soon.'

'How no?'

'Because, you dodo, he'd be incriminating himself! It'd be like admitting he was in her house and he still denies all knowledge of her. Besides, even if he did want to do it, I'll make sure Dunbar enters a plea of self-defence. I just need to hear what he's got to say for himself first. Right, come on, what did you get at McClusky's gaff?'

Oblivious to the question, Duncan wandered to the kitchenette, took a mug from the cupboard, and flicked the kettle on.

'Oi!' said West. 'What the hell do you think you're doing?'

'Making a brew. I've not stopped all day, and I've still not had my lunch yet.'

'Well nor have we! Come on, spit it out!'

Duncan walked to the table, reached for his inside pocket, and produced the two padded envelopes.

'I give you exhibits A and B,' he said as he pushed them towards her. 'One marked "Henry", the other, "Jack". Each envelope contains exactly one thousand pounds in used twenties.'

'And these were in his office?'

'Aye. In the drawer he couldn't wait to close when we arrived.'

'So, what do you reckon?'

'Well,' said Duncan, 'if Jack and Henry were chartering the boat as they claimed, then McClusky's hardly likely to be paying *them* for the privilege, is he? No, no, I'd say it's their fee for services rendered.'

West flashed him a wink and smiled.

'Lunch,' she said, 'is on me. Whatever you want. Egg, bacon–'

'Hold on,' said Duncan, 'by the time I've finished, it's a table at Cecchini's I'll be needing.'

Munro, watching the performance like a proud parent at a prize-giving ceremony, smiled as Duncan pulled up a chair, swung his feet to the desk, and dangled the three sets of keys before them.

'These,' he said, 'are the nails I referred to earlier.'

'I'm listening.'

'Okay, as we know, Tam McClusky no longer drives but Callum does. He's got a wee van he uses for delivering fish.'

'I know,' said West. 'You can smell it up the road.'

'Aye, but here's the thing,' said Duncan, as he waved the fob, 'this is for a Toyota. Callum McClusky drives a Volkswagen Caddy.'

West, unimpressed, stared at Duncan and raised her eyebrows.

'So, it's an old key,' she said, 'big deal. I've got stacks of them.'

'Do you remember that big, white pick-up Jack and Henry Boyd were hosing down outside their house?'

'Yeah.'

'Do you remember the make?'

'I didn't look,' said West. 'I was too busy waiting for them to burst into song.'

'Well, it's a Hilux, miss. A Toyota Hilux.'

West took a seat beside him, cocked her head, and frowned.

'So,' she said as she inspected the key, 'what you're implying is–'

'Aye, exactly!' said Duncan. 'I reckon McClusky owns the pick-up and the Boyds used it when they were on the job.'

'Alright, I'll go with that,' said West. 'We'll have to check it out, but I'll go with it for now. What about the house keys?'

Duncan glanced furtively at Munro and cleared his throat.

'Okay,' he said, holding up the first set, 'tell me if you think I'm losing the plot here, but what do you make of this?'

Dougal leaned forward, squinting as he scrutinised the faded gold and red logo on the metal fob.

'Estrella Damm,' he said. 'Damm's the oldest brewery in Spain and Estrella is probably their best-selling beer.'

'Aye. And what does estrella mean?'

'Oh, that's genius!' said Dougal. 'Pure genius.'

'What is?' said West.

'Estrella, miss! It means star, and the Boyds live on Star Street.'

'Give me strength! That's pushing it a bit, isn't it? Don't tell me you've got a connection between the Boyds and a lucky rabbit's foot as well?'

'No, no,' said Duncan. 'It's nothing to do with the Boyds. And it's not a rabbit's foot, miss. It's *Lendalfoot*.'

'Okay, I've heard enough,' said West. 'It's high time you got some food, a lack of sustenance is obviously playing havoc with your imagination.'

Munro shook his head and smiled.

'I'm disappointed, Charlie,' he said, chuckling to himself.

'You what?'

'You! You should know better! See here, lassie, McClusky's no fool. He's like a fox. He's clever, aye, but he's cunning too. Deceitful. And if you want to catch a fox, then you have to think like a fox. I say hats-off to Duncan.'

'Sorry,' said West, 'am I missing a trick here? I still don't get it.'

'Listen, Charlie, McClusky's not going to do something as stupid as writing the names on the keys, is he? All he's needing is a visual cue to differentiate between the sets. Something only he will understand. To someone like yourself, those wee trinkets are nothing more than a keepsake from his travels, and let's face it, it's not exactly difficult to put his theory to the test, is it?'

'Alright!' said West, surrendering her hands. 'You win! Have it your way. We'll look for the pick-up first and see if it fires up with that key. Then we'll run over to the Baxter's place later this afternoon and give their door a try.'

'What about the Boyds' place?' said Dougal. 'On Star Street?'

'No rush just now,' said West, 'besides, it's flipping miles away and we need to interview Tam McClusky, his brief should be here by now.'

'Can we not have some lunch first?' said Duncan. 'Will I order us some pizza?'

'I'll take mine plain,' said Munro, 'with a thin crust, mind.'

'And I'll have an American!' boomed DCI Elliot as he squeezed his voluminous frame through the door. 'A stuffed crust with extra pepperoni! And get them to throw some of that spicy chicken on the top as well.'

'George!' said Munro with a smile. 'Is a walk along the corridor a part of your exercise routine these days?'

'Jest if you will,' said Elliot, 'but it's a terrible thing to be burdened with a metabolism like mine. Actually, I'm here for a reason. Charlie, I hear you've arrested Thomas McClusky.'

'Blimey, news travels fast.'

'Well, I hope you know what you're doing. Put a foot wrong and he'll hang you out to dry.'

'Have some faith,' said Munro. 'She knows what she's doing.'

'I'm not convinced,' said Elliot. 'Charlie, does the word "jurisdiction" mean anything to you? McClusky lives in Dumfriesshire.'

'With all due respect, sir,' said West, 'his boat, the *Thistledonia*, ran aground on our patch. Aron Jónsson was found dead on our patch. And Rhona Baxter was murdered on our patch. I'd say we're in the clear.'

'And the young fellow? Alex Dunbar?'

'Well, three out of four's not bad. Anyway, we're not charging him with anything. Not yet anyway. I just need to hear his version of events.'

Elliot glanced at the smiling faces around the table and, conceding defeat, winked at Munro as he left the office.

'Call me when the pizza arrives,' he said. 'As you were, Charlie. As you were.'

Chapter 21

Unlike certain members of the legal profession, in particular, those who sought to intimidate the authorities with a shamelessly ostentatious display of the wealth they'd garnered from defending high-profile criminals, the unassuming Gordon Christie, who owned neither a handmade leather briefcase nor a bespoke suit, had, with his thick-rimmed spectacles, balding head, and tatty gabardine overcoat, more in common with Mr. Magoo than a top-flight lawyer.

Ignoring the two detectives as they entered the room, he produced a scuffed A4 notepad from a torn carrier bag, placed it next to a biro on the table in front of him and sat, head bowed with his hands clasped firmly between his legs as McClusky, with a face like thunder, turned his chair to glare at the side of the solicitor's head.

Likening the mismatched duo to a couple of care home cronies about to compile their bucket list, Duncan, stifling a smile, stood by the door with his hands behind his back while West, carrying a brown paper sack, took a seat and stabbed the voice recorder.

'For the benefit of the tape,' she said, 'I am DI West, also present is Detective Sergeant Reid. Would you kindly state your names, please.'

Christie raised a hand to his mouth and coughed politely.

'Gordon Christie,' he said, softly.

'Louder please, Mr Christie, we can't actually hear you.'

'GORDON CHRISTIE!'

'Blimey, that'll do. And you, sir?'

'Thomas McClusky.'

'Perfect. For the record, I should mention that Mr Christie is a solicitor and is here to advise Mr McClusky. Right, let's get cracking, shall we? Mr McClusky, you've been arrested on suspicion of aiding and abetting the illegal import of a banned substance, notably cocaine, into this country. Do you understand?'

Christie, staring at the desk, nodded once.

'I do,' said McClusky.

'And have you anything to say in response to your arrest and the accusation levelled against you?'

Christie shook his head.

'I have not.'

'Good. Now then, we have reason to believe that your boat, the *Thistledonia*, was being used to transport a shipment of drugs from somewhere off the Faroe Isles to an unidentified location along the coast somewhere between Troon and Kirkcudbright. Are you now, or were you, at any time in the past, aware that it was being used for such a purpose?'

Christie nodded.

'No,' said McClusky. 'I was not.'

'Okay. The last people to charter your boat,' said West, 'were two brothers by the name of Jack and Henry Boyd. How long exactly have you known the Boyds?'

Christie glanced at his client, frowned, and slowly shook his head.

'No comment.'

‘Oh, here we go,’ said West. ‘Right, let’s go back a bit, let’s see if we can jog your memory. Not so long ago we had a conversation, you and I, during which you mentioned that Jack and Henry Boyd were long-standing customers of yours, is that right?’

‘I have no recollection of any such conversation,’ said McClusky. ‘No recollection at all.’

With McClusky adopting a predictably obstinate stance, West, aware that there was more than one way to skin a cat, opted to feign a complete lack of interest by picking up her phone and tapping lethargically at the screen.

‘How long have you known them?’ she said with a yawn. ‘Six months. Twelve? A bit longer, maybe?’

‘No comment.’

‘They chartered your boat to go on fishing expeditions, didn’t they? What did they do with their catch when they returned to harbour? Did they take it home or did they flog it on the quayside?’

‘No comment.’

‘What about your son?’ said West. ‘Callum. He’s in the fish trade, did he help them out? After all, they’re good mates. They were at school together.’

‘No comment.’

West turned to Duncan and sighed with a theatrical roll of the eyes.

‘God, this is getting boring,’ she said as she reached into the paper sack. ‘Let’s try something else. For the benefit of the tape I am now showing Mr McClusky two padded envelopes. Do you recognise these?’

‘No comment.’

‘Let me help you out,’ said West as she flipped them over. ‘You see, this one’s marked “Jack”, and this one’s marked “Henry”. Now, before you say anything, we compared the writing on these envelopes to the entries in your ledger and we’re pretty sure it’s the same. It’s your handwriting, isn’t it, Mr McClusky?’

Christie winced, dropped his head, and groaned as McClusky, his cheeks flushing with rage, spun to face the front.

'Where did you get those?' he said, gritting his teeth.

'Oh, so you do recognise them? Finally, we're getting somewhere.'

'Don't play with me, Inspector! I said, where did you get them?'

'Where you left them,' said West. 'In your office. In a drawer. In the bureau.'

'Right! I've heard enough!' said McClusky. 'You've over-stepped the mark, Inspector! Mr Christie will be filing a formal complaint!'

'Really? What for?'

'Entering my property without permission! Removing items without permission! And so help me God, if you forced your way in–'

'Calm down,' said West as Duncan, reaching for his pocket, produced a folded sheet of paper and smiled. 'My fault, I should've said. We've got a warrant. Oh, and by the way, there's no damage to the door, we let ourselves in – we had a set of keys. Callum's keys. So, back to the envelopes, would you care to tell us what's in them?'

'No comment.'

'I thought not. I'll tell you, shall I? Each envelope contains exactly one thousand pounds. Now, I know it's coming up to Christmas but I'm guessing that as far as gifts go, that's probably just a bit too extravagant so, why were you giving Jack and Henry Boyd a grand each?'

Christie took a handkerchief from his breast pocket and dabbed his forehead as McClusky leaned back in his seat with a supercilious grin smeared across his face.

'It's a refund,' he said. 'For their fishing trip.'

'You're refunding them because some scally nicked your boat while they were having their supper?'

'In the scheme of things,' said McClusky, 'it's not different to having a hire car stolen. The fact of the matter is, they followed procedure, they docked in a safe place and the boat was secured. It's not their fault it was pinched.'

'Even so,' said West, 'I have to say it's awfully generous of you, giving them back all their dosh, I mean, considering they were on the last leg of their journey, if they'd booked with anyone else they'd have been lucky to get ten per cent.'

'That's the kind of person I am,' said McClusky, 'generous to a fault. It's all about customer satisfaction.'

'Is it indeed? It's a shame Aron Jónsson didn't know about your policy, he could've saved himself a trip. You know Mr Jónsson, don't you, Mr McClusky? He's a trawlerman, a big bloke with a beard. He's from Iceland. Oh, I forgot to say, he's a drug dealer, too.'

McClusky glowered across the table as Christie closed his pad and slipped it back into the carrier bag.

'This two grand,' said Duncan, 'is that about the going rate for hiring your boat?'

Christie turned to his right, shrugged his shoulders, and slumped back in his seat.

'Aye,' said McClusky. 'It is.'

'So, this business you're in, renting a boat to a few fishermen, it's a lucrative one, is it?'

'It can be.'

'It can be?' said Duncan with a huff. 'Oh, come on! It must be! I mean, by your own admission, that boat's hardly out of the water! Okay, I'm guessing here, but if two grand's the going rate for a ten-day trip, then you must be making what? Sixty? Seventy grand a year? Is that not right?'

'It's not guaranteed,' said McClusky. 'It depends on the weather.'

'Is that so? Well, last year must have been a belter for you, I mean, we had a cracking summer and let's face it, winter all but passed us by.'

'Aye, it was better than average, I'll give you that.'

'Must be quite a life, eh?' said Duncan. 'Just sitting back, doing nothing while the money rolls in. Don't get me wrong, I'm not the jealous type. No, no. If someone hits the jackpot, I'm the first to say, good on you pal, but some folk aren't like that, are they, Mr McClusky? Some folk want a slice of the action, too. Folk like the Department for Work and Pensions and Her Majesty's Revenue and Customs. They'd be raging if they knew what you really earned, especially as you told them that you made less than six grand, which gets me thinking, your mattress must be bulging at the seams.'

Christie buttoned his coat and groaned as if troubled by wind while Duncan perched on the edge of the desk, folded his arms, and stared at McClusky.

'Your son. Callum,' he said. 'He lives with you at home so you must see him all the time but tell me this, Mr McClusky, when did you last see your daughter?'

McClusky, stony-faced, stared directly at Duncan and paused before answering.

'No comment,' he said, emphatically.

'Too late for that,' muttered Christie.

'So, not recently, then? How about Maureen? Have you seen Maureen, or Willy?'

'No comment.'

'How about Callum? Does he get on with his stepsister?'

'No comment.'

'I think he does,' said Duncan. 'In fact, I'd go so far as to say, they get on really well, I mean, why else would she let him use her bank account to launder his drug money?'

'No comment.'

Duncan stood, drove his hands deep into his jacket pockets, and wandered to the side of the room.

'See here, Mr McClusky,' he said, 'I understand the love of a father. I'm a surrogate one myself, so I get that. I get what they'd do for the weans, protect them, come hell or high water. So, tell me, what were you protecting Callum from? Why were you covering for him?'

'I've never covered for him in my life,' said McClusky. 'He's an adult. If he's done something wrong, he can pay the price, just like anyone else.'

'Well, that's admirable,' said West, 'but there must have been something, I mean, why else would you lie about the flu?'

'I've not lied about anything!' said McClusky. 'I told you, the lad had it bad! I took him to the infirmary myself! If you'd done your homework, Inspector, you'd know that!'

'Oh but we have,' said West. 'And guess what? We got a gold star and a tick. Callum went to the infirmary alright, there's no doubt about that, but he wasn't treated for flu, was he? He was treated for stab wounds.'

'That can't have been easy,' said Duncan. 'I mean, a wee hard man like Callum having to get his father to take him to the hospital because he'd been stabbed. Not just stabbed, mind, but stabbed by a girl! His own sister!'

'She didn't stab him!' said McClusky, yelling as he thumped the table. 'It was…'

Duncan glanced at West and smiled as McClusky, catching himself, fell silent.

'That's what I like to see,' he said, 'a wee bit of co-operation. Now, will you finish that sentence or will I?'

'No comment.'

'No bother,' said Duncan. 'See here, Mr McClusky, we know it wasn't Rhona who stabbed Callum. It was her boyfriend but that son of yours must have quite a temper because we know what he did to her later that evening.'

'What are you driving at?'

'You mean to say he didn't tell you? Dear, dear, and I thought you two had some sort of inseparable bond. Murder, Mr McClusky, it can't get more serious than that, and as far as you're concerned, the game's a bogey, pal.

You'll be charged with tax evasion, false accounting, and benefit fraud.'

'Very good,' said McClusky with a smirk. 'I'll pay what I owe and get a slap on the wrist. Now, if we're all done here–'

'No, no,' said Duncan, 'you're not out the door just yet, you seem to have forgotten why you were arrested in the first place. We've the small matter of art and part to deal with but before that, we're away for a wee chat with Rhona's boyfriend so you sit tight. We'll see you in a few hours.'

Chapter 22

Had she witnessed a performance like Duncan's whilst serving as a DS in London, then the younger West – whose demeaning male colleagues perpetually inflamed her sense of insecurity – would, with absolute certitude, have taken it as a non-verbal criticism of her interview technique enacted for the sole purpose of undermining both her confidence and her authority. However, coming from an underling who'd once harboured a blatant disregard for following orders and made a habit of flirting with any suspect of a female persuasion, she couldn't help but feel a tinge of pride knowing that in some small way she'd been responsible for his transformation into a first class, if unconventional, interrogator.

Certain that Alex Dunbar, a timid bundle of nerves at the best of times, would respond more favourably to her questions in the dubious comfort of the Defender than under the menacing gaze of her number two in the cold confines of an interview room, she settled back and waited, beeping the horn as his scrawny silhouette appeared across the car park.

'They're clavering already,' he said, as he hopped into the passenger seat. 'It's not often one of their porters gets his collar felt by the police.'

'Ignore them,' said West. 'It doesn't matter what they think, and you haven't had your collar felt, so relax. At least we've got some privacy here.'

'Right enough,' said Dunbar, 'if we were in the hotel, they'd probably all be listening at the door.'

'Are you alright? It must have been a bit of a shock to learn about Rhona. I'm just sorry it had to come from me.'

'No bother,' said Dunbar. 'I'm fine. I think. I just have to get on with things. With life. I mean, what else can I do?'

'Well, you can help me for a start.'

'How?'

West turned to face Dunbar, stared earnestly into his eyes, and spoke softly.

'I need to know what happened,' she said. 'Between you and Callum McClusky.'

Dunbar drew a breath and twitched nervously in his seat.

'Callum?' he said. 'Sorry, but I don't know anyone called–'

'Alex! Listen to me. We found the knife and it's got your prints all over it, so we can either have a friendly chat here, the only condition being that I might need a sworn statement off you later, or I can run you in right now, charge you with ABH, and let it go before the court. So, what's it to be?'

Dunbar lowered his head and sighed.

'Will there be any comeback?' he said. 'You know, repercussions? Will McClusky come after me?'

'No,' said West. 'He's banged up already, you'll be fine.'

'And my boss? If she finds out, will she sack me?'

'She won't,' said West. 'It's hard to sack someone if they've done nothing wrong. So, what do you say?'

'What do you need to know?'

'Everything. Everything about the night it happened.'

Despite his fears, and an almost debilitating attack of the butterflies, Dunbar, preferring a one-to-one with West in the safety of the car to an earful of abuse from his parents should they discover he'd been arrested for assault, hunched his shoulders and took a deep breath.

'We were watching telly,' he said. '*University Challenge*.'

'Blimey! A bit of a brainbox, then, was she?'

'Aye. Well, she liked to think so. She never answered any questions, mind.'

'So, what happened?'

'McClusky showed up.'

'Just like that?'

'Aye, just like that, out of the blue.'

'Did you recognise him?'

'I've seen him hanging around the hotel a few times, I thought he was a delivery driver or something.'

'And what did you think? About him showing up?'

Dunbar chewed his lip and frowned as he pondered the question.

'I thought it was odd,' he said, 'that some fella should be knocking her door at that time of night.'

'Did it make you jealous?'

'It did. I thought maybe he was an ex or something, but he seemed alright, friendly enough, but…'

'But what?'

'I'm not sure,' said Dunbar. 'Rhona. I mean, she wasn't exactly made up to see him. She seemed a wee bit odd.'

'Not surprised?' said West. 'As in, surprised to see him?'

'No. More nervous, I'd say.'

'And then?'

'She said she needed a wee chat, in private, so they went upstairs to the bathroom.'

'And how did that make you feel?'

'Like a spare part. Like I shouldn't be there. I was going to fetch my coat and leave but…'

'Go on.'

'I couldn't help myself,' said Dunbar. 'I went to the foot of the stairs and tried to listen in on whatever it was they were gabbing about.'

'And did you hear anything?'

'Just muffled voices, but then she sort of screamed.'

'Sort of?'

'Aye, not loud,' said Dunbar, 'it was almost as if they were… anyway, I felt angry and embarrassed, then it happened again, but louder, a proper scream. So, I took the knife from the kitchen and went upstairs.'

'That's not like you,' said West. 'Don't take it the wrong way, Alex, but you're not exactly the kind of lad who'd go steaming into a fight, are you?'

'Maybe not,' said Dunbar, 'but he was shouting too, raging, he was yelling something about an envelope and her father. All I could think was that, if he was hurting her, I had to do something about it.'

'So, what did you do?'

'I opened the door. He had Rhona by the scruff of the neck, I thought he was going to smash her head on the basin so I just lunged at him with the knife.'

'Did he fight back?'

'That's the funny thing,' said Dunbar. 'No, he didn't. Maybe it was shock because he wasn't expecting it. He just swore at me, called me every name under the sun, and legged it downstairs.'

'How did Rhona react?'

'Not happy,' said Dunbar. 'She had a pop at me, too. She told me not to interfere, that it was just some silly argument.'

'And you?' said West. 'How did you feel?'

'I near wet myself. I was shaking. But then Rhona, see, she calmed down a bit. She gave me a wee hug and called me her knight in shining armour.'

'So, she was grateful, after all?'

'I think so, aye.'

'What did you do next?'

'She said we should go out, she said she was hungry, so we walked to the Indian.'

'I can't say I blame her,' said West, 'I think I'd have done the same thing. So, did you have a good night?'

'Definitely not. She hardly said a word and barely touched her food. It was like she had something on her mind, like she was preoccupied, so we went back to the house. That's when she…'

'She what?'

'She changed,' said Dunbar. 'Her mood. She was all anxious, like she was in a panic. She said she had to go, that she was having some time off and she needed a lift.'

'Where was she going?'

'Her parents' house. In Lendalfoot.'

'So, you dropped her there,' said West, 'and did you walk her to the door?'

'No, no. She wouldn't let me. I left her at the bottom of the lane but I waited, mind. I waited until she was safe indoors.'

'Is that why she didn't have any bags?' said West. 'Because she left in a hurry?'

'Maybe. Just her handbag, that was it.'

'I'm assuming, then, that you didn't see her again?'

'No,' said Dunbar. 'The last thing she said before she left the car was that she'd give me a call once she'd got her head together, and that I wasn't to mention anything about what had happened to anyone, anyone at all.'

'And did she keep her promise?' said West. 'Did she call?'

'She did,' said Dunbar. 'Just the once. She said she was going to meet Callum to smooth things over and that she'd see me in a few days and explain everything. Next thing I know, you lot turn up and that's the end of it.'

'Hold on,' said West. 'Sorry, mate, but if she called you, then why wasn't your number on her phone?'

'She called on a landline,' said Dunbar. 'I didn't recognise the number, I just assumed it was her parents'.'

'And that's it?'

'Aye,' said Dunbar. 'That's it. I never heard from her again.'

Despite feeling a hint of compassion for the unlikely have-a-go hero who'd clearly reacted in the best interests of his partner, West, well aware of the risk that he might, at some point in the future, renege on his promise to give a statement, waited until he was halfway across the car park before delving into her pocket, retrieving the voice recorder, and switching it off.

Chapter 23

Unbeknownst to Kay Grogan, who was looking forward to spending a few hours snuggling up to the dashing DS Dougal McCrae in the darkest recesses of a romantic restaurant, her would-be suitor, pandering to her love of the great outdoors, had meticulously planned a rambling woodland walk in the hope that a jaunt in the countryside would be enough to fire her enthusiasm for a second excursion to the Galloway Forest Park where she might enjoy lounging on the banks of Loch Doon in the company of an erudite and pragmatic young fisherman.

However, anxious that should the date be the unmitigated success he was hoping for, it might leave her keen to test the durability of his bed springs, he'd taken the precaution of setting the alarm on his phone for Saturday at precisely 5.17pm thereby saving himself the potential embarrassment of having to fumble with somebody infinitely more experienced than himself by feigning a call to arms.

'Does she know what you've got in store for her?' said Duncan, with a smirk.

'No, no. It'll be a surprise.'

'You're telling me. Do you not think you should warn her?'

'No, why?'

'What if she turns up in a cocktail dress and stilettos?'

'Jeez-oh!' said Dougal, panicking. 'I never thought of that! Do you think she might?'

'Well, if she does,' said Duncan, 'give me a call and I'll happily stand in for you. What about lunch? Have you booked somewhere nice?'

'No! We're away on a walk! I'm taking a packed lunch.'

'Are you joking me?'

'It's no bother,' said Dougal. 'Fish paste sandwiches, a couple of boiled eggs, a bottle of Irn-Bru, and some teacakes for afters.'

'There'll be no afters if you offer her that lot. Listen to me, pal, it's a first date, you need to take her somewhere decent.'

'Really?'

'Aye! Look, go for a walk if you really have to, but if you want my advice you'll take her for a cream tea or a slap-up meal to make up for it afterwards. Push the boat out! Just make sure it's not the *Thistledonia*.'

'Oh, I'm not sure,' said Dougal, 'she'll probably think I'm trying to impress her.'

'Well, you are!' said Duncan. 'Look, you don't have to take my word for it. Chief!'

Munro, standing by the window with his hands clasped firmly behind his back, failed to respond.

'I say, chief! It's dark out, you'll not see anything there but some old fella staring back.'

'Learning without reflection,' said Munro, 'is a waste. Reflecting without learning is dangerous. Confucius.'

'You're confusing me,' said Duncan. 'I said, should Dougal take his lassie to a restaurant or subject her to an SAS assault course in sub-zero temperatures?'

'A restaurant, of course,' said Munro, 'unless you're trained in CPR, in which case, the upside of the latter is that you may get to kiss the girl a wee bit sooner than you expected.'

'Oh, that's it!' said Dougal, his fingers flying across the keyboard. 'I'd best see what's available, I bet they're all booked up!'

'No bother,' said Duncan, 'if the worst comes to the worst, you can grab yourselves a fish supper and head back to your place.'

'I'll cancel. Would she mind if I cancelled?'

'Would who mind?' said West as she lumbered through the door. 'Blimey, that's a pig of a drive, I'm not doing that again in a hurry, it's a right pain in the backside.'

'How was he?' said Duncan. 'Did he come clean?'

'He sure did,' said West, tossing Dougal the voice recorder, 'and I got it all on tape. Download that for me, would you, and keep it somewhere safe. Right, Jimbo, why the long face? Do you need an aspirin or something?'

'No, no,' said Munro, 'physically, I'm fine. It's the mind that's troubling me.'

'Well, I'm sorry, but unless you've got a pot of savings, I can't afford a care home on my own. What's up?'

Munro turned back to the window and gazed at his reflection.

'If Duncan's right,' he said, 'if those keys are for the house in Lendalfoot, then I fear we may be about to uncover some deep, dark secret between Tam McClusky and William Baxter.'

'In what way?'

'It's crossed my mind that perhaps William Baxter didnae happen across the *Thistledonia* by chance. In fact, I'm beginning to wonder if he was there deliberately.'

'What do you mean?'

'I mean, I'm wondering if he was there to meet it.'

'Oh, I'm not sure about that, chief,' said Duncan. 'Have you seen him? He's a poor, miserable sheep farmer with an alcoholic wife. Why would he be meeting some old fishing boat in the dead of night?'

'To retrieve the cargo.'

'Highly unlikely,' said West, jangling the keys, 'but we'll soon find out. Come on, if we get a wiggle on, we can be there and back in an hour.'

'An hour?'

'Alright, two.'

'Have you seen the time?' said Munro. 'If we go now, we'll be late for our supper.'

'Oh, come on, Jimbo. A couple of hours won't kill you, but I might. Tell you what, come with us and we'll grab a takeaway on the way back. My treat, and no washing-up.'

Munro raised a hand to his chin and pondered the proposition.

'A haggis supper,' he said. 'Aye, okay, I could go a haggis supper. Alright, you're on.'

'Good man.'

'But I'm riding with Duncan, mind. At my time of life I'm entitled to a wee bit of comfort.'

* * *

There were times, mused Munro, when the need to arrive at a crime scene or an RTA as a matter of urgency necessitated the use of excessive speed but, with the needle nudging ninety and not so much as a winged pheasant lying in the road, he questioned the reasoning behind Duncan's attempt at the land speed record and shook his head disparagingly when, as if deliberately trying to exacerbate the situation, he killed the headlights before slowing to a crawl and turning off the main road towards the Baxter residence.

Illuminated by the unearthly glow of a December Cold Moon, West, zipping her coat against a snell wind blowing in off the firth, surveyed the house from a distance and concluded that, in the absence of any lights, Mr and Mrs Baxter had either nipped to the supermarket for their weekly shop, or popped into Girvan for a pie and a pint.

'The place is dead,' she said, softly.

'Well, if there's no-one here,' said Duncan, 'why are you whispering?'

'I don't know,' said West, pointing at the dog, 'but it's so flipping quiet, it just seems wrong to shout. Are you bringing him with us?'

'Aye, of course,' said Munro. 'If I leave him in the car he'll get anxious and just start barking, and that would never do. I still cannae see why it takes three of us to turn a key in a lock.'

'Because,' said West, 'you can't be too careful. Some blooming great animal might leap out of the woods, like a wild boar or… or a wolf, then what would we do?'

'Rejoice,' said Munro. 'Rejoice at the reintroduction of Canis lupus to Caledonia after an absence of one hundred and twenty years. Right, on you go, knock the door.'

'What for?'

'To see if anyone's home, lassie! Then you can ask their permission to try the key.'

'Oh, don't be daft,' said West, 'look at the place, it's in total darkness. Duncan, give it a go, but do it quietly.'

Duncan took the first key, slid it gently into the night latch, and gave it a quarter turn.

'It works,' he said, 'but the door's locked.'

'What did I tell you?' said West. 'They're out. Try the Chubb, they must have double-locked it.'

Duncan spun the key in the lock and winked.

'We're in.'

'There's a great deal of satisfaction to be had when your instinct pays off,' said Munro. 'Commendable, laddie. Commendable, indeed.'

'Right, will we go inside?'

'What for?' said West. 'We came to see if the key works, it does, job done.'

'Oh, come on,' said Duncan. 'Just a wee peek, I mean, should we not check they're okay? They might have taken a fall or something.'

'You're having a laugh,' said West. 'Come on.'

'But if they're home, we could ask them about Tam McClusky. Chief, what do you reckon?'

'It's not for me to say,' said Munro, 'but I think you should heed the advice of your…'

Munro smiled as Duncan, ignoring the pair of them, eased the door open and stepped inside to find the house, save for a slither of light beneath the cellar door, swathed in darkness.

'There's a light on downstairs,' he said, lowering his voice. 'Either they forgot to turn it off, or there's somebody down there.'

'No, that doesnae make any sense,' said Munro, 'if there was somebody down there, then why would they lock the door from the inside?'

West, desperate to get her hands on a piece of deep-fried haddock and a side order of mushy peas, brushed by Duncan and, in her own inimitable style, flung open the door to the cellar and stomped down the stairs, shouting as she went.

'Mr Baxter!' she said. 'Willy? It's DI West! Are you there?'

* * *

The room, even down to Rhona's tote bag lying on the ottoman and the crusty bowl sitting on the sideboard, was exactly as she remembered, apart, that is, from the sound of laboured breathing coming from behind the sofa which was inexplicably two feet further from the wall than it should have been.

Spooked by Duncan's prophetic sixth sense and envisaging a comatose Willy Baxter lying flat on his back with a broken hip, West took half a pace forward and paused in disbelief as Maureen Baxter's head appeared from behind the backrest.

'It's yourself, Inspector,' she said, slurring her words.

'How are you, Mrs Baxter?'

'As well as can be… what are you doing here?'

‘I need to ask you some questions,’ said West, as Duncan and Munro made their way down the stairs. ‘Do you want to come and sit down?’

‘Is this about Rhona?’

‘Yup. The thing is, Mrs Baxter, we know who her father is.’

Maureen smiled like a hapless drunk trying to focus on a bottle and eased her way around the sofa as if negotiating a perilous precipice at the peak of Ben Lomond before flopping down with her arms sprawled out beside her.

‘I see,’ she said, her eyes fluttering.

‘Can I get you a glass of water?’

‘Aye, if there’s a wee dram in the bottom of it.’

‘I think you’ve had enough,’ said West. ‘Don’t you?’

‘Just a minute,’ said Maureen, wagging her finger. ‘How did you get in? Did I not lock the door?’

‘You did,’ said West, ‘but we’ve got a set of keys. Tam McClusky’s keys.’

‘What were you doing back there, Mrs Baxter?’ said Duncan. ‘Did you lose something?’

Maureen glanced up and narrowed her eyes.

‘Aye,’ she said. ‘I dropped… I dropped…’

‘What did you drop?’ said Duncan as Murdo shot behind the sofa. ‘By the look of the dog, I’m guessing it was food. A biscuit, maybe?’

‘Aye, that’ll be it,’ said Munro. ‘A few crumbs, perhaps. He’ll soon hoover them up.’

Duncan peered behind the sofa and smiled as Murdo, nose twitching, scratched furiously at the floorboards.

‘No crumbs, chief, but there’s definitely something down there, a wee mouse, maybe. Will I take a look, Mrs Baxter?’

‘Don’t trouble yourself,’ said Maureen, ‘Willy can–’

‘Oh, it’s not trouble,’ said Duncan, ‘the board’s loose, anyway. I’d say if there’s something dead down there, then we best get it out before you’re plagued by bluebottles.’

Maureen stared glassy-eyed at Munro and sighed with the weight of someone drawing their terminal breath.

'Well, it's not a mouse,' said Duncan, 'but I think we best fetch Willy, don't you, Mrs Baxter? Where is he?'

'Up the way,' said Maureen, 'he's hauling feed to the sheep. You'll find him in the bothy if he's not on his way back.'

'Sorry,' said West, 'but would you mind telling me what's going on?'

Duncan rose to his feet and held a small package aloft. A small, silver package wrapped in copious amounts of cling film.

'I think wee Murdo should join the drug squad, miss. He's a nose for it.'

'Right,' said West, 'I'm going to have a chat with Maureen, you two look for Willy and no hanging around, bring him straight back here.'

* * *

Hovering by the kitchen door to the rear of the house, Duncan, allowing his eyes to adjust to the gloom of the night, gradually picked out the form of a shingle path weaving its way between several raised vegetable beds, the outline of a garden shed and, parked by a timber-framed garage, the profile of a large, white car.

'Hold on, chief,' he said, as he pulled a flashlight from his pocket. 'I think I recognise that.'

Directing the beam towards the 4x4 with one hand whilst aiming the Toyota key fob with the other, he gently pressed the button and grinned as the lights flashed in acknowledgment.

'It's the Hilux, chief. The one the Boyds were using.'

'So, this is where he kept it,' said Munro. 'I'll say this for McClusky, he knows how to keep his hands clean, I'll give him that.'

Passing through a five-bar gate, they embarked on the half-mile trudge up a boggy field to the bothy in the distance, Duncan with his hands in his pockets, Murdo on the scent of a badger, and Munro struggling to stay upright as the terrier dragged him along at a pace greater than he was used to.

'I'd say you were right,' said Duncan. 'With all that toot under the floorboards, it looks as though Willy Baxter was out to meet the *Thistledonia* after all.'

'Aye, it would appear so,' said Munro, 'but everything's not always as it seems.'

'How so?'

'His wife, Maureen, she'd not be on her knees behind the sofa unless she had a hand in this herself.'

'Right enough,' said Duncan, 'although there's still a possibility that she wasn't lying, chief. Maybe she did drop something back there and doesn't know anything about the drugs at all, I mean, she's completely hammered, and let's face it, she didn't have the floorboards up.'

'You might be right,' said Munro, 'either way, she'll be needing some coffee before you bombard her with questions. You can give Mr Baxter the third degree while you wait.'

* * *

The bothy, a stone-built affair with a corrugated tin roof, no door, and holes where the windows used to be, had long since seen the likes of weary ramblers or haggard hikers seeking respite from the elements. Instead, the shelter it provided was enjoyed by the sheep that flocked to the ruin every evening for their supplementary feed.

As with most bothies, there were no luxuries to be had, no rooms and no electricity, no taps or running water, no toilet, nor even a fireplace, but this particular one boasted a feature the likes of which Munro had never seen before.

'You'd best call Charlie,' he said, crossing himself at the sight of Willy Baxter's lifeless body dangling from the rafters. 'And an ambulance too.'

Epilogue

Unlike their uniformed colleagues who enjoyed a mandatory work schedule, which, governed by the rules of Health and Safety, restricted them to a forty-hour week with plenty of rest days and overtime at time-and-a-half, for detectives in the force, driven by a vocational desire to secure a conviction and pressurised by a need to collate evidence, question, and then charge a suspect against the clock, any kind of timetable was about as useful as a voucher for an all-inclusive holiday with Thomas Cook.

With her craving for food over-riding any desire to crawl beneath the duvet, a bleary-eyed West popped some bread into the toaster and emptied a tin of beans into a saucepan while Murdo curled up on the couch and Munro, trying his best to stay awake, uncorked the wine.

'Sorry, Jimbo,' she said. 'I shouldn't have dragged you out, my fault entirely. You even missed your haggis supper.'

'No need to apologise, Charlie, it's not necessary.'

'I just didn't realise we'd be out so late.'

'None of us realised we'd be out so late, and none of us expected to find Maureen Baxter huddled over a stash of cocaine or her husband dancing like a puppet from the rafters.'

'Yeah, there is that, I suppose. It's beans on toast, I'm afraid.'

'Perfect,' said Munro as he raised his glass. 'Your very good health.'

'Cheers,' said West. 'Well, that's the weekend out the window, or Saturday at least.'

'It's not easy being a detective, lassie.'

'Maybe, but it is quite good fun, in a twisted kind of way.'

'I'll not disagree with that,' said Munro. 'So, tomorrow, interviews and paperwork, I assume?'

'Yup, Duncan's coming in so it shouldn't be that bad.'

'Not Dougal?'

'Nope. He's got his hot date, remember?'

'Well, you best keep quiet about the Baxters, lassie. The lad's so nervous he'll probably jump at the chance of skipping his date in favour of the safety of the office.'

'Well, if he does show his face,' said West as she served supper, 'then trust me, I'll be on the phone to Kay Grogan like a shot and I'll be inviting her over for lunch. He's not getting off that lightly, it wouldn't be fair. The girl's crazy about him.'

'She'd have to be,' said Munro. 'So, Maureen Baxter. What's the story?'

'Sorry?'

'Your wee chat! She must have said something while we were looking for Willy.'

'That,' said West, 'is an understatement. It was like a blooming therapy session. Once she'd started, she couldn't stop. She just blurted it out like she'd been bottling it up for years.'

'And had she?'

'Pretty much, yeah. In fact, that's probably why she likes a drop of the hard stuff.'

'So?'

'Well,' said West, as she glugged her wine, 'where do I begin? Tam McClusky. He's had her under his thumb ever since he discovered Rhona was his daughter.'

'Did he not know she was his?'

'Nope. He didn't have a clue until Maureen told him. It seems she and Willy were having a rough time of it a few years back. They were all but skint so she went cap in hand to McClusky thinking as Rhona was his daughter, she'd get some money out of him.'

'And did she?'

'She certainly did,' said West, 'but in the process, she backed herself into a corner. McClusky made her a proposition and told her that if she didn't accept, then he'd have no choice but to tell Willy Baxter about their little secret.'

'So that's how she became involved,' said Munro. 'Dear, dear, that being the case, Charlie, you can throw coercion at him as well.'

'Oh, don't you worry, I certainly will. The good news is, she's willing to testify and that will be enough to put him back behind bars for a very long time indeed.'

Munro pushed his plate to one side and topped up the wine.

'So, how did it work?' he said. 'Did she not give you a wee insight into their operation?'

'According to Maureen,' said West, 'McClusky had planned the whole scheme while he was banged up for the armed robbery. That's where he got his Icelandic contact from. Maureen pitching up with news of his daughter was what you might call serendipitous.'

'I'm intrigued, lassie. Go on.'

'When McClusky got out he set about reinventing himself as a pillar of the community. He bought the boat, the *Thistledonia*, and sat on it for nearly two years, renting it out to punters who wanted to go fishing. Then, with his reputation sealed, he set the wheels in motion. Callum got in touch with Henry Boyd who, as we know, already had form, and made him an offer he couldn't refuse.'

'You mean he threatened him?'

'No!' said West. 'He offered him the chance of making a shedload of cash for doing nothing but sail a boat up the coast and back. As soon as the Boyds agreed, McClusky gave them the money to buy the dinghy and the Hilux, which they did through their company, and that was it, they were up and running.'

Munro went to the kitchen and returned with a plate of cheese and crackers in one hand, and the bottle of Balvenie in the other.

'Who was he selling to? He must have had a list of dealers as long as your arm.'

'He did,' said West. 'I'm hoping we'll find out who they are after another Q&A session with the man himself. I've got a feeling McClusky isn't the kind of bloke who'll enjoy going down alone.'

'And Willy Baxter? I have to say, Charlie, I'm surprised a fellow like that agreed to get involved.'

'He didn't,' said West. 'The poor sod knew nothing about it.'

'Are you joking me?'

'Nope. He really did come across the *Thistledonia* by accident. It was Maureen who went to meet the boat and pick up the drugs. It was timed to perfection. They'd wait off-shore until Willy was on the evening shift with the sheep, then the Boyds would scoot out in the dinghy, bring the merchandise back to dry land, and Maureen would take it to the house and stash it beneath the floorboards in the den.'

'Who'd have thought a chap like Baxter could be so naïve?'

'He wasn't. Not entirely. He knew something was up but he couldn't quite place his finger on it. Until they saw the news, that is, a couple of days ago. That's how they found out McClusky had been arrested.'

'And then?'

'And then,' said West, 'they had the mother of all arguments and Maureen went into meltdown. She figured she'd be banged up for life if the cops found out so she told Willy everything. Unfortunately, the poor sod put two and two together and came up with eight.'

'How so?'

'He thought he'd be done as well. Guilty by association. And he reckoned if the press found out then that'd be it. Everyone would know about the drugs, but what hurt him most of all, was that they'd also find out that Rhona wasn't his daughter and, as Maureen said, he couldn't stand the shame or the embarrassment, or the prospect of dying in jail.'

'So, that's why he decided to end it all,' said Munro, shaking his head. 'It's a tragedy, lassie. You couldnae make it up.'

'I know,' said West. 'If only he'd waited and not been so rash, he'd have found out that he wouldn't be charged with anything at all. He'd have been in the clear.'

'Still not much of a future,' said Munro. 'Without his wife he'd have been left alone with all the rumours and the gossip hanging over his head. Frankly, I cannae blame the chap for doing what he did. I'd have probably done the same.'

'Don't be daft,' said West, 'you're too, well, sensible. The irony of it all is that when McClusky finally pops his clogs, there'll probably be more people at his funeral than there'll be at Willy's.'

'McClusky? A funeral? I'm telling you, Charlie, even landfill's too good for that fellow. What about the lassie, Rhona? Did you get to the bottom of that?'

'Eventually,' said West, reaching for the Balvenie. 'When I spoke to her boyfriend, that Alex Dunbar bloke, he mentioned that Callum McClusky had been raging about an envelope. Well, guess what? Maureen had it. She found it in Rhona's bag and it was stuffed with cash.'

‘I’m not with you, Charlie. What does Callum’s cash have to do with it?’

‘Alright, concentrate,’ said West, ‘this is where it gets interesting. Remember I said I thought he was laundering cash through Rhona’s bank account?’

‘It was a fair assumption to make, aye.’

‘Well, he wasn’t. That cash was Rhona’s fee for helping him out.’

‘In what way, Charlie?’

‘Callum was flogging pocket-sized parcels of coke off the back of his fish van. Little, plastic bags shoved down the gob of some unsuspecting halibut, and somehow he had to justify his income. So, he forced her to provide him with advice slips to balance against his fake invoices to the hotel.’

‘So you’re saying he wasnae a supplier at all?’

‘Nope. Dougal had a shufty at his paperwork,’ said West. ‘It’s rammed with invoices addressed to the hotel and against each one is a fake payment slip for cash to that amount. Dougal double-checked with the hotel and it turns out they’ve never heard of him. They get all their fish from a wholesaler in Stranraer.’

‘Why did she not simply refuse?’ said Munro. ‘From the off? She could’ve said, I’m not getting involved.’

‘Simple,’ said West. ‘He threatened her. Or rather, her family. He said he knew where they lived and he’d go after them if she didn’t help him out.’

‘And I’m assuming,’ said Munro, ‘that thanks to his father, he was armed with plenty of detail about Willy and Maureen Baxter and what they did for a living.’

‘Exactly,’ said West, ‘but as with most things in life, there came a point when she thought enough was enough, and I reckon that’s why they had that argument in the bathroom. She wanted out and he wasn’t having any of it.’

‘And that’s why he killed her?’

‘Yup. Inadvertently maybe, but killed her all the same. Dunbar can verify from a phone conversation he had with

Rhona that Callum went to Lendalfoot to meet her, presumably to get his money back. I'm filling in the blanks a bit here, but I'm guessing she claimed not to have it so he was driving her back to Stranraer to pick it up when they must have had another wing-ding in the car and that's when he flipped, gave her what for, and tossed her in the burn.'

'I feel a lesser charge of manslaughter coming on.'

'Funnily enough,' said West, 'that's exactly what McClusky's lawyer, Gordon Christie, is pushing for. The sad thing about it, Jimbo, is I don't think Rhona went home for a holiday. I think she went to keep an eye on her folks.'

Munro took his tumbler of whisky to the sofa, sat next to Murdo, and crossed his legs.

'It's not much of a weekend for you, Charlie. Have you any plans for Sunday?'

'Nah, not really. Duncan thinks I should give Andy McLeod a bell and invite him over for lunch.'

'That's not such a bad idea,' said Munro, 'the distraction will do you good.'

'Maybe, but to be honest, I can't be arsed with all that small talk and having to be polite. I'm too tired for all that. What about you?'

'Och, well, we'll head back to Carsethorn in the morning. Then I imagine we'll be walking, sleeping, and eating.'

'Is that it? Just you and Murdo?'

'Well, who else would there be?'

'Me,' said West. 'I could come over. We could do your garden, it probably needs a bit of weeding.'

'It does, aye.'

'Well, there you go. You can't do that on your own. We could have a roast to make up for your haggis supper. A blooming great rib roast with all the trimmings.'

'You mean vegetables?'

‘I mean spuds. Roast potatoes, tons of them. What do you say?’

Munro drained his glass, smiled at West, and winked.

‘I’d say that’s a capital idea, Charlie. Aye, that’s the word, capital.’

Character List

JAMES MUNRO (RETIRED) – Almost back to full health, aided in no small way by Murdo, his rescued Scottish terrier, the irrepressible James Munro offers his opinion on a convoluted case and sets the team running in all directions.

DI CHARLOTTE WEST – Now a force to be reckoned with, the headstrong Charlie West, taking a lead from her mentor, starts to follow her instinct rather than the facts or the rulebook, and reaps the rewards in more ways than one.

DS DOUGAL McCRAE – Wired to the internet with a nose for sniffing out the smallest of details, the technologically minded DS McCrae finally finds a kindred spirit in the form of a young scenes of crime officer but his nerves threaten to end the date before it's started.

DS DUNCAN REID – The maverick DS, whose appearance alone is enough to have suspects quaking in their boots, hones his skill at bending the rules to within a fraction of breaking point, much to the delight of the retired James Munro.

DCI GEORGE ELLIOT – The ebullient DCI Elliot, who protects his team with the fervour of a patriarch, finds himself reluctantly questioning West's unorthodox methods when handling a cross-border investigation.

DR ANDY MCLEOD – Forensic pathologist Andy McLeod, who spends more time in the company of cadavers than in the land of the living, has his work cut out when the bodies start rolling in.

THOMAS (TAM) McCLUSKY – An altruistic and affable ex-con who, having served his sentence, enjoys a stress-free lifestyle dividing his time between the café, the betting shop, and the harbour where he charters his fishing boat to the hordes of tourists keen to experience life on the high seas.

JACK BOYD – The joint owner of a small construction company who, when offered the chance to boost their turnover with a contract based on a gentlemen's agreement, seizes the opportunity with both hands.

HENRY BOYD – With a conviction under his belt and a knack for lifting more than just bricks and mortar, Henry Boyd, the fearless brawn behind his brother's brains, will stop at nothing to protect their family interests.

WILLY BAXTER – Riddled with guilt over personal inadequacies and plagued by suspicions of his wife's infidelity, the downtrodden sheep farmer has his life ripped apart when he uncovers a treacherous secret.

MAUREEN BAXTER – The doting housewife falls foul of the bottle when her enthusiasm for love, life, and the great outdoors is soured by a ghost of the past.

RHONA BAXTER – An effervescent hotel worker whose bubbly lifestyle takes a turn for the worse when she becomes inadvertently embroiled with a local drug dealer.

CALLUM McCLUSKY – A dockside fishmonger with a reputation for being as slippery as the eels he plies off the back of his van.

ALEX DUNBAR – A kitchen porter whose dalliance with an older woman sends his moral compass into a spin.

KAY GROGAN – An alluring scenes of crime officer with a passion for fishing, forensics, and the diffident DS Dougal McCrae.

If you enjoyed this book, please let others know by leaving a quick review on Amazon. Also, if you spot anything untoward in the paperback, get in touch. We strive for the best quality and appreciate reader feedback.

editor@thebookfolks.com

www.thebookfolks.com

ALSO BY PETE BRASSETT

In this series:

SHE – book 1
AVARICE – book 2
ENMITY – book 3
DUPLICITY – book 4
TERMINUS – book 5
TALION – book 6
PERDITION – book 7
RANCOUR – book 8
PENITENT – book 9
TURPITUDE – book 10

Other titles:

THE WILDER SIDE OF CHAOS
YELLOW MAN
CLAM CHOWDER AT LAFAYETTE AND SPRING
THE GIRL FROM KILKENNY
BROWN BREAD
PRAYER FOR THE DYING
KISS THE GIRLS

SHE

With a serial killer on their hands, Scottish detective Munro and rookie sergeant West must act fast to trace a woman observed at the crime scene. Yet discovering her true identity, let alone finding her, proves difficult. Soon they realise the crime is far graver than either of them could have imagined.

AVARICE

A sleepy Scottish town, a murder in a glen. The local police chief doesn't want a fuss and calls in DI Munro to lead the investigation. But Munro is a stickler for procedure, and his sidekick Charlie West has a nose for a cover up. Someone in the town is guilty, will they find out who?

ENMITY

When it comes to frustrating a criminal investigation, this killer has all the moves. A spate of murders is causing havoc in a remote Scottish town. Enter Detective Inspector Munro to catch the red herrings and uncover an elaborate and wicked ruse.

DUPLICITY

When a foreign worker casually admits to the murder of a local businessman, detectives in a small Scottish town guess that the victim's violent death points to a more complex cause. Money appears to be a motive, but will anyone believe that they might be in fact dealing with a crime of passion?

TERMINUS

Avid fans of Scottish detective James Munro will be worrying it is the end of the line for their favourite sleuth when, battered and bruised following a hit and run, the veteran crime-solver can't pin down a likely suspect.

TALION

A boy finds a man's body on a beach. Police quickly suspect foul play when they discover he was part of a local drugs ring. With no shortage of suspects, they have a job pinning anyone down. But when links to a local business are discovered, it seems the detectives may have stumbled upon a much bigger crime than they could have imagined.

PERDITION

A man is found dead in his car. A goat is killed with a crossbow. What connects these events in a rural Scottish backwater? DI Charlotte West investigates in this gripping murder mystery that ends with a sucker punch of a twist.

RANCOUR

When the body of a girl found on a mountainside tests positive for a date rape drug, police suspect a local Lothario is responsible. He certainly had the means, motive and opportunity. But is this really such a cut and dry case? What are the detectives missing?

PENITENT

The shady past of a small town surfaces when a young woman is found murdered in a pool. As detectives investigate, a legacy of regret and resentment emerges. DI Munro and DI West must get to the bottom of the matter.

TURPITUDE

A murdered jeweller, a series of bungled moped robberies and several fingers found at a refuse site. What connects these events? That's what DI Charlie West and her team must find out, with a little bit of help from Munro. But will the latter be too distracted by his new friend to be of much help?

Made in the USA
Las Vegas, NV
22 February 2021